Madison is a spy, or at least he's supposed to be. He's not inclined to spy on the people who saved his life and report to the woman who almost killed him, but he might not have a choice if he wants to save his sister.

Tyrian doesn't expect to like playing babysitter to the wolf shifter who almost died in a fire, but for some reason, he's fascinated by Madison, especially after Madison comes clean and tells him he's supposed to spy on the pack.

Madison is caught between a rock and a hard place, which seems like the worst place to fall in love, yet here he is. Who would have thought he'd ever trust a vampire enough to fall for him?

Tyrian always trusts his instincts, and they're telling him that Madison is The One. That's enough for him to believe it, but he knows nothing will be easy for them.

The pack has too many enemies, and they're all ready to kill.

Loyal Fangs
Copyright © 2023 Catherine Lievens
ISBN: 978-1-4874-3962-0
Cover art by Angela Waters

Published by eXtasy Books Inc

Look for us online at:
www.eXtasybooks.com

Loyal Fangs
Life with Fangs 11

By

Catherine Lievens

CHAPTER ONE

Madison's world was reduced to pain and fear. Those were the only things he could feel, and while he was trying to fight his way through it for Katie, he didn't know if he could. It felt too big and like it would swallow him and never let him out.

He deserved it. After what he'd done, it made sense that he'd end up in hell. It didn't matter that he was still alive — this was hell, and he didn't think he'd ever leave it.

The world around was burning. He'd tried to stop Fay and the others, even though he'd known it would be useless. He was correct, and now he was going to die here, in this burning building.

He tried to push himself forward for Katie because she didn't deserve to lose the only person who cared about her, but he couldn't. Something had fallen on top of him, and even though he was a wolf shifter, he was too weak and in too much pain. He wouldn't be able to force away whatever that something was, and he'd burn to death under it.

When a sharp pain rose from his legs, he sucked in a breath and got a lungful of smoke. He coughed, his lungs burning so badly he was surprised he wasn't on fire.

Yet.

But it wouldn't be long. He prayed for death because he needed to get away from the pain. It was too much, and he didn't know how to deal with it without screaming. He doubted anyone would hear him, but Fay had set fire to this place for a reason, and it wasn't to kill Madison. She wanted someone to attempt to save him and get hurt, and he wouldn't give her the satisfaction. He wouldn't take other wolf shifters down with him as he died.

The only sound Madison could hear was the whoosh of the fire until something caught his attention. It was a distraction from the pain and fear, but unfortunately, it wasn't enough to forget them. He tried to blink, unsure of what he'd see, but his eyelids felt like sandpaper on his eyes.

He was stunned to realize two people were coming toward him. He didn't know where they'd come from or who they were, but this was his only chance to make it out of there. He felt like he deserved to stay and die, but he couldn't do that to his sister. He couldn't abandon Katie with their father.

That meant he had to live.

When the people reached him, he raised a hand. He couldn't see much with the smoke around him, but he almost cried when the two men leaned down to grasp him. That hurt, too, but it meant he wouldn't die, and that was all he wanted.

They hauled him to his feet. He cried out at the pain racing through his body, but he needed to focus on Katie. Who cared if he was in pain as long as he was alive? He'd be fine. He had to be.

He was terrified of looking at himself. He didn't want to see how burned he was and what his body had been reduced to. Would he scare Katie? Would he ever see her again? He had no idea who had grabbed him except that he was pretty sure they were both guys, which meant that he might still be in danger of dying if they decided he was too much bother or an enemy.

Maybe that wouldn't be such a bad thing.

The pain was so harsh that he couldn't breathe—although that might be because of the smoke. He wanted to die, but Katie had already lost too much. She didn't deserve to lose him, too, especially in these circumstances.

One of the men leaned down. For a second, Madison didn't understand what he was doing. Then two arms wrapped around him. He was hauled up into the man's arms, and he screamed.

"Sorry," the man whispered, his voice barely audible over the sound of the fire.

Madison could only nod, but he was starting to wonder if it was worth it. He was in so much pain that he doubted he could have a normal life after this, and not just because of the fire. He was part of something he'd never wanted to be part of, and he didn't know how to get out of it or even if he could. Maybe it would be easier for everyone if he just died here.

But he wasn't going to be allowed to do that. The man rushed toward the exit, not wasting time. Madison had no energy to speak, so he leaned against the guy's shoulder. Even through the fire, the man smelled good, and Madison found himself thinking that it wouldn't be too bad to die like this.

A loud creaking sound made him glance up. A flash of heat and a loud sound caused him to cringe back, but the guy who held him just cradled him closer. He carried Madison out of the building as if the fire couldn't touch him.

Maybe it couldn't. Madison didn't know much about dragon shifters, because he felt better staying as far away from the clan as possible, but they were dragons and spat fire. This was probably a walk in the park for dragons.

These guys couldn't be part of the clan. The clan didn't have a reason to save Madison. If anything, they wouldn't hesitate to leave him in the building to die. They might be allied with Fay, but that didn't mean they were friends or that they would shed a tear at the news that one of her shifters had died.

The heat suddenly vanished. It was so much of a shock that it took Madison a moment to realize why he couldn't feel it anymore. He blinked up at the sky, his heart tripping over itself.

He was out. Maybe he wouldn't die after all.

He tried to move and changed his mind. He could still die from the pain and burns, but at least he wouldn't be alone. Maybe he'd even get to see Katie one last time.

"What's your name?"

It took Madison a moment to realize the man carrying him was talking to him. He opened his mouth, wondering if he'd be able to speak. "Madison." His voice was little more than a croak, but he could speak, and the words tumbled out. "I swear, I told them I didn't want to be involved. I wasn't okay with this. I tried to stop them, but I couldn't. I—"

Madison needed to stop talking, but he didn't know if he could. If he was going to die, the pack needed to know what was happening and what Fay was planning. Otherwise they'd be destroyed, and Madison's home would be gone.

"Who did this?" the other man asked.

Madison was glad that man wasn't carrying him, because he was intimidating. He was so tall that Madison had to tilt his head back to look at him, and his expression was stony. It told Madison that this man wouldn't hesitate to hurt him if it meant protecting the people he loved. The fangs that peeked from the man's upper lip as he spoke were another reason Madison realized he was in trouble. He needed to explain himself, but he was about to die. He just knew it.

"Fay gave the order," he whispered. "I never wanted to hurt anyone. I never wanted to leave the pack."

There. Now the pack would know what Fay was doing. They'd know she was behind all of this, and hopefully, they'd be able to defend themselves.

Madison's heart hurt at the thought of his sister being stuck with Fay and their father, but there was nothing he could do. Maybe if he had enough energy, he could beg these guys to save his sister, but why would they do that? Why would they help the sister of a traitor? The daughter of one?

"Madison?"

Madison's eyes burned. For a moment, he wasn't sure what he was seeing. Then he realized Kieran was standing there. His hand was held out as if he'd been about to touch Madison but had stopped before doing so, and when Madison looked down, he realized why.

He wasn't sure his arms would ever recover from this.

He swallowed and tried to convince himself this wasn't his body, but the pain wouldn't let him deny it. The skin of his arms was a deep red in some places, black in others.

"I swear I didn't want to do this." Madison wanted the alpha to believe him. Maybe if he did, he'd help Katie even after what Madison had done. She was a child and didn't deserve to be left where she was. "That's why they left me inside to die. I tried to convince them to stop, but Fay has too much control over them." The words came out in a rush, and Madison wasn't sure they made sense. He just needed Kieran to know.

Tyrian's heart broke a little at the pain and fear in the man's voice. He wanted to step in and help, but it wasn't his place, so he stayed where he was. Kieran had things in hand, and he was the alpha.

Tyrian wasn't sure what Kieran would do. From what the man in Arlen's arms had said, it was clear he'd been involved in the fire. It was also clear he hadn't wanted to be and that he'd tried to leave. His people had almost killed him, and something told Tyrian they wouldn't hesitate next time.

What they'd done was almost worse. They'd abandoned him in a burning building. They'd left him to die there, in pain and terrified, and the thought of that made Tyrian want to hunt them down and kill them. He wasn't usually bloodthirsty, but he couldn't stand it when people did something so cruel.

"We'll have time to talk later," Kieran murmured. "Merrick and Arlen will go with you to the hospital. They'll keep an eye on you until I can come and get you. I want to believe you, but I don't know if I can trust you."

The words gave Tyrian a jolt. Of course Kieran didn't know if he could trust Madison. Madison had just admitted he'd been with the group that had set the building on fire. He might be horribly burned, but that didn't mean he was telling the truth. He probably wasn't. Having someone infiltrate the pack as a victim would lead Kieran to lower his guard. Maybe Madison was a Trojan horse. Maybe he was here to open the way to Kieran's sister and the clan.

Madison sobbed. "I just want to come home," he whispered. A tear rolled down his cheek, leaving a clear path in the soot covering it.

Tyrian had to resist the urge to reach out and dry it. He didn't want Madison to cry.

"You will," Kieran told him. It sounded like a promise, and it seemed to soothe Madison.

He relaxed in Arlen's arms, and his eyes fluttered shut. He needed medical help as soon as possible, and Tyrian wanted to tell Arlen to move. But he wasn't the one giving orders, and he reminded himself of that once again.

"Arlen and I would be more useful here," Merrick said.

Tyrian didn't know Merrick well yet, but he could hear the anger in his voice. He was furious with Madison, which made sense, but maybe it would be better if he didn't take Madison to the hospital.

Tyrian cleared his throat. "Merrick is right. As dragons, he and Arlen can do a lot of good here. On the other hand, I'm just a vampire. I can take care of Madison while they focus on the fire."

Kieran stared at Tyrian for a moment. Tyrian thought for sure he'd say no, and he wouldn't have blamed him. They might be kind of a family now, but they hadn't known each other for long. The general mistrust between shifters and vampires also didn't help.

"If you're sure it's not a bother," Kieran eventually said.

"I wouldn't have offered otherwise. Just tell me what you want me to do."

Kieran nodded. "We have several people who work at the hospital. They'll be able to help him without letting anyone know he's a shifter."

That was vital, since the world didn't know about shifters and vampires, and it was better to keep things that way.

"I'll call them as soon as you leave here so they know you're on your way," Kieran continued. "Just keep an eye on Madison. I don't think he's on Fay's side, and I want to believe everything he said, but I don't know if I can."

"I'll stay close," Tyrian promised.

He agreed with Kieran. Madison was too frightened and in too much pain to be lying. Maybe he'd been recruited to set the building on fire, but he clearly hadn't been okay with doing so, and he'd paid for that.

He'd paid for attempting to do the right thing and stopping the arsonists. It wasn't fair, and Tyrian promised himself he'd do what he could to help Madison recover. That still didn't mean Madison wasn't a spy, which meant they'd need to keep an eye on him, but for now, as far as Tyrian was concerned, he was as much a victim as the pack.

Madison clearly wouldn't get far, even if he tried running. Tyrian might not have been inside the building when Arlen and Merrick had found Madison, but he had eyes. He could see how much damage the wolf shifter had sustained, and healing wouldn't be easy or quick, even though he was a shifter.

Arlen was gentle as he transferred Madison into one of the cars Tyrian and his family were using at the moment. They'd left their vehicles behind when they'd come to the pack, but eventually, they'd have to make a decision. Could they stay here forever, living with a wolf pack, or would they head home?

That wasn't a question Tyrian wanted to think about now. If the pack was in danger, so was Mallory, one of the men Tyrian had turned into a vampire and considered family.

As soon as Madison was in the back of the car, Tyrian drove off. He could hear Merrick still talking to Kieran and pointing out that Madison might be a spy, but even if he was, he wasn't going anywhere right now. Tyrian felt protective of him, which wasn't a surprise. There was a reason he'd gathered such a big family, and that reason was that he never wanted anyone to be in pain. He had a soft heart, and when he couldn't help the people he found wounded or hurt, he turned them into vampires, as long as they were okay with it. He'd saved the people he now considered his children, and maybe, he could save Madison, too.

Although he doubted Madison would want to be turned into a vampire.

"I never wanted any of this," Madison suddenly said from the backseat.

Tyrian wouldn't have heard him if it weren't for his vampire senses. "How did you end up caught in it, then?"

"I was forced. I never wanted to leave the pack. It's my home, and I don't want anything to do with the dragons." Madison coughed, then winced. "I think Kieran is a good alpha, even though he let vampires in."

"You shouldn't be talking. Your lungs are probably full of smoke," Tyrian pointed out, even though he wanted to continue listening to Madison. But Madison's voice was hoarse, and Tyrian didn't want him to hurt himself even worse just to apologize.

"I just need you to know that I never wanted any of this. I'm not a bad person."

"I didn't think you were."

Tyrian doubted Madison was involved in what Kieran's sister was plotting. Well, he was in some ways, since he'd been found there, but Tyrian didn't think Madison was a spy. Even if he'd been left behind so the pack would save him and he could spy on them, it wasn't a mission he'd volunteered for.

Either that or he was an excellent actor who deserved an Oscar.

Tyrian was relieved when they reached the hospital. Several people were waiting for them in front of the entrance, and they whisked Madison away. Tyrian wanted to go with him, if anything because he'd promised Kieran he would, so he followed, his phone already in hand to let Kieran know they'd arrived.

He was allowed to sit in a corner of the room where Madison was being treated. He didn't know how long he sat there, listening to Madison's cries and whimpers, but the sounds made him want to throw up. He knew pain and fear and what feeling both was like, yet he wasn't prepared. It sounded like they were torturing Madison rather than helping him, and it took everything Tyrian had not to lash out. He wanted to drag the doctor and the two nurses away from Madison.

But he didn't. Instead, he got to his feet and went to stand just outside the room. He was surprised to find Meyer was there, leaning against the wall. Meyer was one of his children, a member of his family, and it was good to have him there.

"How's it going?" Meyer asked.

"Horribly."

Meyer's expression was grim. "I heard. Do you think he's going to make it?"

Tyrian thought about Madison's big, soulful brown eyes. "I hope so."

Madison had never felt so much pain. He thought he'd already reached the limit a human being could stand, but he was wrong. This was worse. This made him want to scream and push away the hands touching him.

It made him want to die.

"It's done," someone said as they lightly touched his forehead.

He blinked open his eyes. He felt like he couldn't understand the words, so he stared at the person standing by his bed.

It was the vampire from before who'd brought him to the hospital. Why was he still here? Was he planning on eating Madison?

"He should start healing fast now that we cleaned the wounds and burns," someone else said.

Madison rolled his head to look to the other side of the room. The doctor wore a white coat, and Madison remembered him. He was a pack member and had stayed with Kieran when Fay had decided to leave. She'd been angry because of that. She knew her pack would need a doctor, but they wouldn't get the one she felt belonged to them.

"Unfortunately, he'll have scars, especially on his arms," the doctor continued. "His legs should be fine, because they were protected by whatever fell on them."

"But he'll be fine?" the vampire asked.

"He will. I wish I could keep him here longer, but someone will notice how fast he's healing. I can't afford for that to happen."

The vampire nodded. "I'll take him to pack territory. I called Kieran, and he told me to do so."

"Good. I'll be able to check in on him once I come home. He needs rest and food."

"I'll take care of him."

Madison didn't understand why the vampire promised that. Was it only because Kieran had asked him to? There couldn't be any other reason, yet Madison found himself hoping for one.

No one knew he was gay. His father would have killed him if he'd found out, and Madison hadn't wanted to risk losing his sister. Because of that, he'd never told anyone, and he hoped that his reaction to the vampire wouldn't make it obvious.

But he couldn't look away. The vampire was so incredibly handsome and looked out of place in the hospital. He was older than Madison, although Madison didn't think by much. How was he supposed to know, anyway? Vampires didn't age, so he could be a hundred years old.

But no matter how old he was, the vampire was incredibly good-looking. Even after the fire, his brown hair was neatly combed, and there wasn't a speck of dirt on his clothes. His blue eyes captured Madison's attention, and Madison wondered what it would be like to have those eyes focused on him.

He found out after a few moments because the vampire turned to him. "I'll carry you out to the car," he murmured.

Madison wanted to protest that he could walk, but he wouldn't mind another opportunity to be in the vampire's arms. Besides, he wasn't sure he *could* walk. He couldn't feel his legs and was afraid to look down at them. The doctor had said his legs would be fine, but they didn't feel like it at the moment, and that was terrifying.

"I'll come by to check the burns once my shift here is over," the doctor said as he stepped aside to give the vampire space "Just make sure he rests and eats. No showers or anything like that."

Showering was the last thing Madison was thinking of doing right now. The nurses and the doctor had cleaned him up as well as they could without shoving him under a showerhead, and even though he still smelled like smoke, that was perfectly fine with him. He felt like he might break down if he showered, and he could only imagine how much it would hurt his arms.

He wasn't looking forward to finding out.

"I'll follow your instructions," the vampire promised.

"Good. I'll hold you responsible if anything happens to him, Tyrian."

Madison smiled. Now he knew the vampire's name. He still didn't know who the vampire was, but he didn't feel that mattered. Kieran trusted him, which meant Madison could trust him, too.

Once he was in Tyrian's arms, he leaned his head against Tyrian's shoulder. Tyrian didn't seem to mind as he carried him out of the room, then out of the hospital. Madison was already almost asleep by the time they reached the car, and he let Tyrian manhandle him into the passenger seat.

Pain spiked in his arms with every movement, but the doctor had said it was a good thing. It meant the nerves still worked and that Madison wouldn't lose sensation in his arms. Right now, he kind of wished that wasn't so, but he knew that once he started healing, he'd be grateful.

Tyrian was silent as he started driving. Madison pressed his forehead against the cool window of the car and looked outside, but his eyelids kept sliding shut no matter how hard he tried to resist.

He didn't know how long it took, but eventually, the car stopped. He opened his eyes, sucking in a breath at the sight that greeted him.

He would have recognized pack territory anywhere. The

sensation of being home was overwhelming, and he had to fight the tears that threatened to fall. He was a mess and didn't know how to deal with any of this.

His father would have slapped him and told him to act like a man. Madison would have obeyed to avoid being beaten and so Katie wouldn't see him cry. She wasn't here now, though, and neither was his father. Tyrian probably wouldn't care if Madison cried. They didn't know each other, and while Madison didn't understand why Tyrian had volunteered to be his babysitter, he was glad.

"What happened?" someone asked as soon as Tyrian opened his door.

Madison tried to sit up, but he was drained. He didn't know if he could take a step, let alone go wherever Tyrian wanted to take him. Thankfully, he didn't have to worry about it. Tyrian was already opening his door and helping him out of the car, then hauling him up into his arms and cradling him close.

"Was anyone hurt?" another voice asked.

It sounded like a bunch of people had gathered and wanted answers. Madison was afraid to see who was there, so he closed his eyes and snuggled against Tyrian.

"I don't know anything," Tyrian explained. "Kieran sent me home with Madison after he was burned."

"What's he doing here?" the first voice asked.

Madison screwed his eyes shut. He didn't want to see who sounded so angry. They were right to feel that way.

"He was wounded," Tyrian said.

"You should have left him there to die."

"Stop," Tyrian ordered. "None of you know the circumstances of what happened to Madison, and I won't let you hurt him. I have clear orders from Kieran, and I'll follow them. You should, too."

There was a moment of silence, and Madison held his

breath. It didn't matter how powerful a vampire Tyrian was. If even two wolf shifters attacked him, he'd get hurt, and Madison didn't want that to happen.

"Fine," the second voice said. "But we're not happy about any of this. He's a traitor, and he shouldn't be here. He left the pack."

"You'll have to talk to Kieran about this. I'm just keeping an eye on him while he heals."

Tyrian started moving. Madison continued leaning against him. He could feel it when Tyrian climbed steps, then opened a door. The sound of another car parking behind them almost made Madison open his eyes, but he didn't care who was there. He just cared about how safe he felt in Tyrian's arms.

At this point, he didn't even care if Tyrian tried to eat him. His father insisted that vampires only thought about blood and were little more than animals guided by their instincts, but Madison knew that wasn't true. He'd known it before, of course, but the fact that Tyrian wasn't trying to eat him was proof of it.

Or maybe Tyrian enjoyed hunting and wanted Madison to get better first.

Madison huffed at his thoughts and looked up at his savior. That got Tyrian's attention, and he looked down, a brow arched in question. Madison closed his eyes again, not knowing how to answer the silent question.

"There's an empty room," a new voice said.

"I should put him in mine," Tyrian answered.

"You'll need to be away from him eventually. You can't watch him forever."

"Kieran asked me to keep an eye on him."

"For now. I'm sure Kieran will want to move him once he comes back. Put him in the guest room, Tyrian. There's no need for you to fret over him."

The words made Madison want to throw up. Maybe the

second man was right, and there was no need to fret over Madison. It wasn't like anyone ever did, anyway. His mother had died when Katie was born, and since then, Madison hadn't mattered to anyone but his sister.

That wasn't going to change anytime soon.

Madison didn't want to think about how terrified and confused Katie had to be. She was ten, and she understood much more than Madison wished. She knew he didn't want to obey Fay when Fay had chosen him for this mission, and she would know something had happened to him when he didn't return. There was no way for him to reassure her that he was okay. Hopefully, Fay would lie.

She knew what had happened to Madison, since he was here to spy on the pack for her.

He gritted his teeth. He wasn't going to do it, especially after what Fay had done. He'd tried to stop her from burning down the building and told her it wasn't necessary and that he could sneak back into the pack without it. She hadn't listened. She wanted revenge and didn't care who she hurt in the process. The pack members who'd stayed with Kieran would pay as much as he would, and she'd make sure of that.

Madison had told her he didn't want to spy, but she'd threatened Katie, knowing that would give him no choice. She'd hurt him and told him that it would look more realistic this way. She had no idea he wasn't planning on sneaking around. She was holding his sister's life over his head and believed he'd do anything to protect and save her.

She was right. Madison *would* do anything to save Katie. But going along with what Fay was planning wasn't the right way to do that.

Tyrian didn't understand why he wanted to keep Madison close, but he couldn't deny that Meyer was right. He needed a private place to rest, and having Madison in his room wouldn't help. So he took him to the guest room, relieved that it was next to his room. That way, he could hear if anything happened to Madison.

"You can't save everyone," Meyer said as he followed.

Tyrian looked down at Madison. He wasn't sure Madison understood what was being said around him. He was in shock and in pain, his body heavy in Tyrian's arms. "He doesn't need to be saved," he murmured.

"Are you sure about that? Because to me, it looks like he does."

"I'd think you'd want me to help him."

Meyer shrugged. "I don't think that telling you not to do it is going to work. You've always had a soft heart, Tyrian. I wouldn't be here otherwise."

He was right. Tyrian had always had a soft heart, and for some reason, that heart had latched onto Madison. Maybe it was because of how much pain Madison was in or how desperate he'd sounded earlier when he'd tried to explain what had happened. Whatever the reason, Tyrian wanted to protect him.

He usually listened to his instincts. They hadn't guided him wrong often, and he didn't see why they would start now. Something about Madison made Tyrian want to trust him, even considering the circumstances. Few people would understand, but he didn't care about that.

Meyer opened the door of the guest room and stepped aside. Tyrian walked in and headed straight to the bed, where he gently lowered Madison.

That jolted Madison into action. He looked around with wide eyes, his arms clinging around Tyrian's neck. It had to hurt, but either Madison didn't notice, or he was too afraid to care.

Tyrian sat on the edge of the mattress so that Madison

wouldn't hang from his neck. "There's no need to be afraid," he murmured. "Meyer isn't going to hurt you, and neither is Kieran."

Madison blinked, then quickly snatched his hands away. "I know he won't. He's a good alpha."

Tyrian nodded. "He is. Is that why you wanted to come home?"

"I never wanted to leave. My father forced me and my sister to go with him, and I knew he'd hurt her if I didn't agree."

There seemed to be so much more to Madison's story. Tyrian wanted to ask questions and find out what that more was, but he wasn't sure it was his place. Kieran should be here, at the very least. He needed to know the entire story, and it would be better if he got it from Madison.

"I'm sorry to hear that. Well, you're safe now. I can't make promises when it comes to your sister, but I'm sure Kieran will want to ensure she's all right."

Madison's brown eyes were still wide. "Why did you volunteer for this? Are you going to eat me?"

Tyrian almost smiled. He wasn't surprised that a wolf shifter was wary of his reasons for helping. Even the pack members tended to give him and his family a wide berth. They didn't entirely trust them yet, but that would eventually change.

Madison had been taken away from the pack, and he hadn't had the opportunity to meet Tyrian yet. Considering the kind of person his father seemed to be, it wasn't surprising that he'd told Madison vampires would try to eat him.

Tyrian was tempted, but not in the sense Madison was asking.

He shook those thoughts away. The last thing Madison needed was for Tyrian to lust over him. "I don't drink from people without their consent," he explained.

Madison frowned, then winced, probably in pain. "But I

thought that was what vampires did," he argued.

"We're not all the same. I have no doubt that some vampires are cruel and take what they need without asking, but it's not the kind of person I am or the kind of people my family is. I'm not going to bite you without your consent, Madison. I promise you that, and that I won't hurt you."

Madison didn't look convinced, but that was okay.

Tyrian's phone vibrated in his pocket. He took it out, not surprised to see Kieran's name on the screen. He and Meyer looked at each other, and Meyer nodded. He leaned against the wall and crossed his arms over his chest while Tyrian got to his feet.

"I'll be right back," he told Madison before stepping out into the hallway.

He answered the phone as he walked into his bedroom, closing the door for some privacy.

"How is he?" Kieran asked.

The alpha sounded tired, but then, he no doubt was. "The doctor said he would be fine. He'll have scars, but he's already healing." Thank god for that.

It was good that Madison was a shifter, because it meant he'd heal much faster than a human would have. His body was sturdier, which was probably why he hadn't died. From what the doctor had said, though, it had been close, and for some reason, the thought made Tyrian's heart flutter in panic.

He didn't want Madison to die. There was no reason for him to feel that way, but he couldn't deny that was how he felt.

"Good," Kieran said with a sigh. "I don't know what to do with him. Merrick's convinced he's a spy and that he'll run back to Fay as soon as he has the information he needs, but I'm not sure that's true."

"Are you asking me what I think?"

"I suppose I am. You're a leader, too, and you have much

more experience than I do."

That might be true, but at the moment, that experience was clouded by Tyrian's strong feelings for Madison. He wasn't sure he could be objective, but he'd try.

"If I were you, I'd keep in mind that he could be a spy. Don't decide anything before talking to him at length. Ask questions, try to find out why he's here. You can make decisions once you have all the information."

"I guess you're right. I just don't know if I can spare people to keep an eye on him. The fire is still burning, and rebuilding is going to be a bitch."

"I'll stay with him," Tyrian offered because he wanted to keep an eye on Madison, but not just that.

He also wanted to make sure Madison wasn't hurt. His fellow pack members hadn't seemed happy to see him earlier, and Tyrian doubted that would change anytime soon. In their eyes, Madison had betrayed them. They didn't know there was more to it, or maybe they did and didn't care.

From the way Madison had spoken about his father, he clearly feared the man. That hadn't developed over a few weeks or even months. That had taken years, which meant that Madison's father had probably been hurting him for a long time. People tended to notice those things, which meant the pack had probably known about it.

Yet they blamed Madison for leaving.

It made Tyrian angry, but he told himself to relax. He'd have time to talk to Kieran about all of this once they knew the entire story behind Madison's decisions and what had happened. In the meantime, Tyrian would stay with Madison.

"It would be a relief to know you're with him. I trust you more than I trust some of my pack members, at least with him, so it would be good to know no one's going to hurt him."

"I won't let them," Tyrian promised.

"I know. You might not be an alpha, but you're a good

leader to your family, and I trust you."

That touched Tyrian more than Kieran could probably understand. "Thank you."

"Don't thank me yet. This is going to be a cluster fuck."

Tyrian agreed, but he was right in the middle of it, and there was no getting out.

Not without Madison.

CHAPTER TWO

The guest bedroom was nice. It was nicer than the home in which Madison had grown up and definitely nicer than the motel where he and the other shifters who'd followed Fay were currently living. It had been abandoned for a while, so they'd taken over several rooms, but it didn't have electricity or running water. It was the worst place in which to raise Katie, but Madison was the only one who cared about that. Their father didn't care about her at all, which was why Madison had been surprised when he'd insisted Katie come with him when he left. Madison had hoped he'd leave Katie with the pack, and he would have stayed with her.

But no. Madison's father had dragged her along, and now she lived in that rat-infested place. Madison's heart broke at the thought, and he had to fight the urge to get out of bed and try to run back there.

He wasn't going anywhere. Tyrian had left him in the bedroom and locked the door, telling him he was headed to take a shower. Madison desperately wished he could take one, too, but he didn't think he had the energy to get out of bed. His legs felt like jelly, even though the doctor had said they were okay. His arms weren't, and the thought of warm water on the burns made Madison's stomach churn. What he needed was sleep, but he'd been fighting it since he'd arrived. He needed to talk to Kieran as soon as the alpha was back, and he wouldn't be able to do that if he was asleep.

But Kieran wasn't coming. Madison could see the sky from where he was on the bed, so he could tell the sun was rising.

Surely the fire was under control by now. But what if it wasn't? What if it had taken the buildings around it? What if half the town was on fire, and it was all Madison's fault?

Madison's mouth tasted foul, possibly because he hadn't eaten anything in hours or maybe because he felt guilty. It didn't matter. Nothing mattered except talking to Kieran, and he wasn't there.

Madison knew what to do. He felt like he was going to throw up, but he still twisted around on the bed until his bare feet could reach the floor. He pressed them against the cool wood, trying to tell himself that he could do it, even though he didn't believe it. He felt like he would tip forward if he tried getting to his feet, but he had to. He needed to do something.

He tried not to use his hands or his arms. He'd been given painkillers, but his arms still hurt, and he suspected they would as long as they weren't healed. He didn't know how long that would take but hoped it wouldn't be too long. He needed to get back to Katie.

But he wasn't even sure he'd be allowed to.

His legs wobbled when he pushed himself to his feet, but he managed not to fall. He took a tentative first step, then another, moving until he was in front of the door. That was where things turned even more difficult. He didn't know how to get someone's attention, and the only thing that came to mind was to pound on the door. He was pretty sure his arms wouldn't be okay with that, which might be a problem.

He decided to try anyway. Avoiding looking at his arm, he raised a hand, and even though it was bandaged, he knocked.

Every knock jarred his arm and made it ache. He was going to regret this later, but for now, he could do it for a while.

"Hello? Can anyone hear me?" he called out.

He couldn't hear anyone in the house. He knew Tyrian was close by taking a shower, but that was it. Was Tyrian the only one who lived here? He hadn't been alone when he'd brought Madison in, but Madison hadn't recognized the man with him. He was pretty sure the man was a vampire, like Tyrian, and he hoped he wouldn't be the one to open the door.

But he was desperate to have anyone open it, and at this point, he'd even take a vampire he didn't know. He needed someone to do something about Katie, and soon.

He knocked again. "Hello?" he called out again. His voice was still hoarse, and it hurt to yell, but he didn't care.

The sound of footsteps made him take a step back. He stumbled and had to grab the dresser not to fall, which made his hands and arms hurt even worse. He swore and tried to decide what to do. He should go back to bed if someone was coming for him, but he wasn't sure he could. Maybe it would be better for him to cling to the dresser until someone could help him.

He didn't want people to see him like this. He also didn't want to be a burden, so it would be better for him to get back to bed by himself. But even though it was just on the other side of the room, it felt like it was miles away.

He still pushed away from the dresser and headed toward it.

When the door opened, he'd wobbled halfway there. He jolted in surprise and started turning around, but with his arms and legs hurting, his balance wasn't the best. He felt himself tilting sideways, his eyes wide as he watched the vampire at the door.

It wasn't Tyrian but the vampire Tyrian had been talking to when he and Madison had arrived here. Madison was pretty sure he'd seen this vampire at the hospital, too, but he couldn't have sworn so.

The vampire was fast. He was at the door one second, and the next, he grabbed Madison's waist. Madison let out a relieved sigh as the vampire manhandled him toward the bed.

He'd been careful not to touch Madison's arms.

"What are you doing out of bed?" the vampire asked.

"I need to talk to Kieran."

The vampire helped Madison sit on the bed, then took a step away. "He'll come once he's back in pack territory."

"He still isn't back?" What was happening in town? Had the fire been that bad?

Madison had nothing to do with the fire. He'd been trying to stop Fay from setting it, but she hadn't listened. She thought it would be the perfect way for him to go undercover. She'd wanted him to be hurt, and he was.

Part of him thought she'd also wanted to burn down the building because it belonged to someone who hadn't followed her when she left the pack. Her pride was wounded, and she didn't care who she hurt as long as her brother was one of those people. It was awful, but the only thing she wanted was revenge.

"You need to stay in bed. Tyrian will kick my ass if he finds out you've been wandering around the room."

Madison looked up at the vampire. "Why? It's not like you can force me to sit down."

The vampire shrugged. "He won't hear that, though. When he decides to rescue someone, he's focused."

The words made Madison's stomach churn. He hadn't expected Tyrian to find him special by any means, but knowing he was one of many people Tyrian had rescued made him feel bad. "Does he do this often?"

The vampire stared at him for a moment. "More often in the past. Not as often in recent years, although maybe that's changed. I'm Meyer, by the way."

"Madison."

"I know. Well, Madison, I don't know when Kieran is coming home or what he's planning, and I can't let you wander out of this bedroom."

Madison tried to grab the blanket he was sitting on, but his fingers hurt. He winced and dropped his hands to his thighs, unsure where to keep his arms when they were so painful. He didn't want to make things worse by moving too much. "I need someone to let him know I have to talk to him," he begged.

"Tyrian is almost done with his shower. I'm sure he can contact Kieran for you, but we can't be sure Kieran will come."

"That's fine." It was better than nothing.

The sound of a door opening and closing made Madison perk up. He didn't think it was the front door, because the sound was too close, but it might be.

Tyrian appeared. His hair was still damp, and even though it was morning and he and the other pack vampires would probably head to bed soon, he wore a pair of dress pants and a shirt. The shirt was open at the collar, exposing his throat, and Madison couldn't look away.

"What's going on here?" Tyrian asked, looking from Madison to Meyer.

Madison moved his gaze up to look Tyrian in the eyes. "I need to see Kieran. I need to tell him everything."

Tyrian had no idea what was happening, but he didn't like it. Madison needed to rest, and Meyer had no place in the bedroom talking to him.

Tyrian narrowed his eyes at Meyer, who rolled his. "He was knocking on the door. What was I supposed to do?"

"You shouldn't have left the bed," Tyrian gently scolded Madison as he moved closer.

Madison was sitting on the edge of the mattress, but he slid toward the middle of the bed when Tyrian stepped closer. It was almost as if he was afraid, but Tyrian wasn't sure about that. Madison didn't look afraid. Wary, yes, but mainly, he looked like he wanted to eat Tyrian alive.

"I was trying to get someone's attention," Madison explained quickly. "I need to talk to Kieran. It's important."

"I'm sure it is, but Kieran isn't home yet as far as I know. You also need to rest."

Madison shook his head. "I don't. The only important thing right now is talking to the alpha. Please."

Tyrian was hesitant. Kieran had told him to call if anything happened, and this would qualify. Madison's urgency could mean he had a good reason, so it would be better if Tyrian called the alpha.

But if he did, Kieran would come and talk to Madison. That meant Madison wouldn't get any sleep, which he desperately needed. His arms had to hurt, and he didn't look steady, even though he was sitting down.

Tyrian wanted nothing more than to push Madison to the bed and wrap himself around him so he could be sure Madison wouldn't get up again. He could stay there until Madison fell asleep, then maybe prepare some food for him. All of that was incredibly domestic, and that wasn't something Tyrian was used to thinking about. He didn't know why Madison was different, and he didn't care.

"I understand you want to talk to Kieran," he said slowly. "But he's still in town."

"Do you have any news about the fire?"

Madison seemed terrified to find out what was happening, and Tyrian didn't blame him. Fire was one of the worst things that could happen to someone. Losing everything was like a punch to the stomach, and even though the building that had burned down was a business rather than a private home, it wouldn't be easy for whoever it belonged to. Kieran had mentioned it was one of the pack-owned businesses, but while it might belong to the pack, someone had lost everything they'd worked for.

And it might be Madison's fault.

"I don't know much except that it's still raging," Tyrian said gently. "Why don't you tell me what you need to tell Kieran? That way, I can decide whether or not I should call him and ask him to come visit you." It would be useless to tell Madison to go to sleep. He probably hadn't slept yet, and Tyrian didn't think he would until he saw Kieran. It wasn't good for him, but there was no way for Tyrian to force him.

Madison licked his lips and looked at Meyer. Thankfully, Tyrian didn't have to ask Meyer to leave. Meyer nodded, then gestured toward the door. "I'll go and get some food for Madison. Is there anything you don't eat?"

Madison blinked at him. "Do you care?"

"I wouldn't have asked if I didn't."

Madison shook his head. "I eat everything. I'm just surprised you asked, since I'm a prisoner."

"I don't know that you are."

Madison looked confused and turned to Tyrian.

Tyrian gestured at Meyer to go, and he waited until the door had closed behind him to move in front of the bed. "You're not exactly a prisoner. Kieran told me to keep an eye on you, but that doesn't mean you're a prisoner. He just wants to be cautious."

Madison's eyes were wide. "Well, I should be a prisoner."

"Why don't you tell me what's going on? How did you find yourself in that fire?" It was clear Madison wanted to talk, and while he wanted to speak to Kieran, hopefully, Tyrian would be the next best thing.

Madison's lower lip trembled, and he looked down at his hands. His gaze snapped back up almost instantly as if he'd been surprised by the sight of the bandages. Maybe he was, although Tyrian couldn't understand how. He had to be in extreme pain, and if Tyrian were in his place, he wouldn't want to do anything but sleep and forget about the pain. Instead, Madison was fighting to be heard, and Tyrian felt that it was the least he could do for him.

"Fay, Kieran's sister, wanted someone to spy on her brother. She wants to know what's going on with the pack, so she decided to send me." Madison chuckled darkly. "I'm pretty sure my father convinced her to do that. He never liked me, so it wouldn't be a surprise to find out he wanted to get rid of me. He probably thought Kieran would kill me on sight or something."

Tyrian wasn't surprised by anything Madison was saying. He was sorry Madison's father was an asshole, but it wouldn't be the first time someone had been hurt by one of their parents. It wasn't fair, but that was life.

"But Fay knew he wouldn't, because that's not how he is," Madison continued. "I told her I'd just come back and tell Kieran I was sorry and never meant to leave the pack. She felt that wouldn't be enough. She was almost giddy when she ordered me and a few others to follow her. She had a plan, but I swear I didn't know what that plan was."

Tyrian didn't think he'd known. Who would agree to something like that? "She brought you to the business you burned down?"

Madison looked away toward the window. "Yeah. I didn't know why we were there, but they were all excited. I knew it wouldn't be good, and when I realized what they were planning to do, I tried to stop them. I told them that Kieran would let me back into the pack even without the fire and that he wouldn't trust me if I was found there. That's when Fay said that he would if I was wounded."

Tyrian was torn between the instinct to move closer to Madison and comfort him and the instinct to go out there and find Fay. She needed to pay for what she'd done, and not just to Madison.

"Someone hit me on the back of the head," Madison said, reaching for his head before wincing and dropping his hand back to his lap. "I wasn't fully unconscious, so I saw when they started the fire. I tried to get out when they left, but something fell on my legs, and I couldn't move. Before she went, Fay told me to be a good spy and let her know every detail I thought was important." Madison sucked in a breath. "She said that if I didn't, my sister would be the next one to end up in a fire."

Tyrian gritted his teeth. He couldn't snap, especially not at Madison. "How old is your sister?"

"She's ten." Madison smiled, and his entire demeanor changed. "She's incredibly smart, and she's going to do great things."

"I'm sure she is."

"She's the only reason I went with him when he left. He couldn't force me to come, but he knew that by taking Katie away, I would." Madison finally looked at Tyrian again. "The only reason I agreed to spy on Kieran and the pack is my sister. We both want to come home. We never wanted to leave in the first place. But even if Kieran doesn't want me to return, he could take Katie, right?"

Tyrian didn't know how to answer that question. "She's still with your father?"

"She is, but I can go and get her. I don't want Kieran or anyone else in the pack to put themselves in danger. I'll do anything Kieran wants as long as he agrees to take Katie back. Please. I need to talk to him."

Kieran hadn't been the alpha for long, so there was no way for Madison to know what kind of leader he was. From what little he'd seen, though, Kieran was a good person. He'd been a good man while growing up, even though it hadn't been easy with his father. He'd stepped up when it'd become obvious that his father would never be a good leader, and almost everyone had been hopeful that things would finally change for the better.

That was when Madison's father had taken Madison and Katie away. But Madison had hope, and until he saw more of Kieran, he'd hold onto that hope. It was the only thing he could do.

"I'll call Kieran," Tyrian said.

Madison could have kissed him. "Thank you."

"Don't thank me yet. I can't make any promises when it comes to Kieran, and *he* is the alpha." Tyrian hesitated. "But I can promise you that even if Kieran declines to help your sister, I will."

Madison frowned. "Why? You're not a wolf and don't owe me anything."

"I wouldn't be able to live with myself knowing that I left a little girl in the hands of people who might hurt her. It doesn't matter that she's the daughter of a traitor. I'm not a pack member, and that won't be enough to hold me back."

Kieran might be a new alpha, but he wasn't cruel. He'd try to get Katie back, no matter who her father was. Madison had to believe that.

Madison was a different kettle of fish. He was an adult, and while he hoped Kieran would understand why he'd gone along with Fay, that didn't mean he'd be able to forgive him. He might not be allowed to return to the pack, which would destroy his heart, but he'd survive. He was doing all of this to save his sister. As long as she was safe, he'd be all right.

But it wasn't something he needed to focus on now. There was nothing Madison could do. The ball was in Tyrian's court, and he'd be the one to decide what would happen next.

"I'm going to call Kieran and check on Meyer. You need rest and to eat," Tyrian repeated.

Madison shook his head. "I only need to talk to Kieran."

"I don't think the doctor will be happy when he finds out you haven't listened to what he told you."

Madison narrowed his eyes. "I'll rest after I talk to Kieran."

Tyrian seemed almost surprised. Until now, Madison had been meek and gone along with whatever Tyrian and the others told him. This was important to him, though, and he was ready to do pretty much anything to save his sister, including disobeying Tyrian and Kieran. It didn't matter that he was exhausted and terrified and that Tyrian was a vampire Madison didn't know, and that he could kill him easily.

But Tyrian didn't kill Madison. Instead, he smiled.

Madison blinked, surprised, and leaned back at the sight of the fangs in Tyrian's mouth. Tyrian seemed to realize he'd startled Madison and pressed his lips together, and Madison regretted it. He didn't care about the fangs. He didn't care that Tyrian was a vampire. The fangs didn't scare him.

Much.

"I'll be right back," Tyrian promised.

He stepped out of the room, but he didn't go far. It seemed that Tyrian wanted him to hear the conversation, because he put it on speaker and left the door open, but Madison didn't understand why he hadn't just stayed in the room in that case.

"Yes?" the alpha said when he answered.

He sounded exhausted, and Madison felt guilty because it was his fault.

"I'm sorry to bother you," Tyrian told him.

"Not a problem. The fire is under control, and I'll be able to come home soon. How's Madison?"

"Pretty banged up, but he'll heal."

"That's good."

There was relief in Kieran's voice, as if he cared what happened to Madison. It gave Madison hope, but he told himself not to lean too much into it so he wouldn't be disappointed later if Kieran decided he couldn't help him. As long as he helped Katie, Madison would get what he wanted, which was all that mattered.

"Madison has been insisting on talking to you," Tyrian explained.

"I want to talk to him, too, but I don't know if I can do that tonight. I'm exhausted, and I'm surprised he's not asleep already. Didn't the doctor give him something for the pain?"

"He did. But Madison told me what happened, and I understand why he wants to talk to you."

Kieran groaned. "I'm not going to be happy, am I?"

"I don't think anyone would be, considering what Madison told me. He said he was sent by your sister to spy on the pack."

He quickly went through the entire explanation. He told Kieran that the only reason Madison had agreed to go along with Fay's plan was his sister, which was a relief. Madison was glad Kieran would already know what had happened, even though he'd no doubt have more questions for Madison.

"Dammit," Kieran swore once Tyrian was done. "I knew this had something to do with Fay, but I never expected her to threaten a child."

"Madison sounded quite desperate. I don't want to believe someone would hurt a child, but I don't know your sister."

"I thought I knew her, but clearly, I was wrong. Okay. Let me talk to a few people here, and then I'll come talk to Madison. Tell him to rest in the meantime. Hopefully, talking to me means he'll be able to go to sleep once he's done."

"Your doctor won't be happy to find out he hasn't slept yet."

"My doctor can kiss my ass."

Tyrian chuckled. "I see."

"Maybe you do. Right now, the only thing that matters is the pack, and while I want Madison to recover, it's clear he has something important to tell me. I'll be right there."

Even though it hurt, Madison had gotten up while Tyrian was on the phone. He had to know what was being said so he'd know what was coming. He turned to move back to the bed, thankful this was over, at least for now.

He hobbled his way there and was sitting again when Tyrian returned with a tray. The food wasn't much, just a sandwich, but Madison was starving, and it tasted like heaven. He ate quickly, doing his best to ignore Tyrian watching him.

By the time he was done eating, Kieran had finally arrived, and he wasn't alone. Robin, his partner, was there with him.

"Hi," Robin said gently when he and Kieran were in front of Madison.

Madison was fearful, even though he knew he had no reason to be. When Tyrian moved to leave, though, panic gripped him. He didn't know why he trusted Tyrian more than he trusted Kieran, but he did.

Thankfully, Tyrian seemed to understand what Madison was silently asking, and instead of leaving, he leaned against the wall by the door. His presence was enough for Madison to calm down and be able to focus on Kieran and Robin.

"I don't want to spy on the pack, but I didn't have a choice. I had to agree," Madison said in a rush.

"Tyrian told me about your sister," Kieran said. He moved slowly as he sat on the mattress next to Madison, almost as if he was afraid to spook Madison. "I understand why you agreed to go along with her plan even if you didn't want to. I'd do pretty much anything to save the people I love, so I won't blame you for doing the same."

Madison's eyes filled with tears. He didn't want to cry, but he wasn't sure he could stop himself. "I didn't want to leave the pack, to begin with. Katie didn't, either, but she's only ten, so our father forced her to. I knew I'd never see her again if I let them leave, and I couldn't allow that to happen. She's just a child and doesn't deserve what my father would do to her."

The silence in the room was heavy. "What do you mean?" Kieran asked, his voice soft but filled with anger.

Madison tried to make himself smaller. "My father started beating me when I was younger than Katie. I never wanted him to hurt her, so I'd redirect his anger every time he got angry at her. I don't mind being hit if it means she won't be, but if I'm not there anymore, eventually, he'll hurt her."

And Madison never wanted that to happen. He was also terrified of what Fay might do. She had no use for a child, and eventually, she'd want to get rid of Katie. Madison's father wouldn't care. He never did.

"He's the one who told Fay I'd come spy on you," Madison continued. "He volunteered me, and I couldn't say no."

"I wouldn't have expected you to. What do you need from me, Madison?"

Madison clearly didn't know how to answer that question because he looked lost. "I need to call Fay. She told me to call as soon as I could to let her know I was in."

"You have a cell phone with you?"

Madison shook his head. "She said I'd be able to find one."

Tyrian wondered how she'd expected Madison to do that. She'd abandoned him in a building that had been set on fire. What would have happened if Madison had died?

Tyrian didn't want to contemplate that possibility. He was already too protective of Madison, but he didn't care. He needed to keep Madison safe.

Kieran looked at Robin. From what Tyrian had been told, Robin's arrival in the pack was what had pushed Fay to leave, or at least she'd used Robin as an excuse. He knew the story of how Kieran had become the alpha in his father's place. It was clear there was bad blood there. Maybe Fay was angry that Kieran had pushed her father out of the role, or maybe she wanted it for herself. Whatever reason she had for opposing Kieran, it was closely linked to his new role as the alpha.

Robin nodded and moved toward the door. "I'll find a burner. I'm sure the team has one somewhere."

He left, leaving Madison alone with Kieran and Tyrian. Tyrian couldn't look away from Madison. The man was exhausted, and Tyrian wanted to tell him to stretch out and close his eyes. He was tired, too, but there would be no going to bed for him until this was over. He didn't know how the situation would end, but however that was, he'd be there for Madison.

He didn't say anything out loud. He might barely know Madison, but he could already tell the man was stubborn when it came to his sister. That meant that Madison would tell him to fuck off if he suggested the man try to sleep, and it was better not to provoke him, considering everything.

Kieran got up from the bed and moved toward Tyrian. They didn't leave the room, but even stepping away from Madison gave them some privacy, especially after his eyes started sliding shut as soon as Kieran wasn't next to him.

"What do you think?" Kieran asked.

Tyrian was touched that the alpha was asking him for his opinion. Tyrian might be a leader, but his family were the only people he'd ever led. That was nowhere near the same as being the alpha of an entire wolf pack, yet Kieran had never made Tyrian feel like his opinion didn't matter. Tyrian was glad Mallory had found such a good group of people to live with.

He'd been stunned when Mallory had told him he'd fallen in love with a wolf shifter, but also worried. That was why he'd been relieved when Mallory had asked him and the others to come and help the pack. That way, he could keep Mallory safe and ensure the pack wouldn't hurt him.

They wouldn't. Tyrian wouldn't say the pack had welcomed him and his family with open arms, but while they were hesitant and understandably wary, they also weren't hostile. The ones who might have been had left, which meant the vampires were safe with the pack.

"I believe him," Tyrian said softly. "He's terrified for his sister. Of course, you know him better than I do, but I don't think he's lying."

"I don't think he is, either." Kieran peeked at Madison. "I never knew his father was hurting him."

"Would you have stepped in if you'd known?" Because Tyrian wasn't entirely convinced that no one had known. It wasn't possible.

Kieran hesitated. "I want to say yes, but I don't know. My father would have lost his shit if I'd tried something like that, and when he was still the alpha, his word was law. He might have known what was happening to Madison, but even if he did, he wouldn't have seen anything wrong with it."

"Was your father abusive with you and your siblings?"

Kieran shook his head. "He never hurt us physically."

Which didn't mean he hadn't abused them in other ways. Tyrian didn't ask because it wasn't his place, but he understood the situation better now. He supposed that even if people had known what was happening to Madison, they wouldn't have been able to do anything. Stepping in would have meant attracting the alpha's anger, which no one wanted.

It didn't take Robin long to come back. When he did, he was carrying a phone that he handed to Madison. Madison hesitated, then tentatively smiled at him. Robin smiled back.

Tyrian could tell Madison was wary of vampires, so it was good to see him comfortable with Robin, considering Robin was his alpha mate. Not everything was lost, after all. If they managed to get Madison's sister back, Tyrian had no doubt the pair would be able to make a home here with the pack.

Kieran sat on the bed again. Tyrian wanted to be the one next to Madison, but this was better. He didn't want to spook Madison, and Kieran was Madison's alpha, so he was the one who should support him during this.

"We'll keep quiet so she doesn't know we're here," Kieran explained. "Do you already know what you're going to tell her?"

Madison shook his head. "Just that I'm in and that I want to know how Katie is."

"Good. Don't tell her you were honest with me. I'm hoping we can use this to our advantage, maybe by giving her false information."

"I won't do anything that puts Katie in danger," Madison warned.

"I don't want anything to happen to her, either. We'll only do it if it's safe for her, all right? But we need to find a way to get to her, and that won't happen if you tell Fay that you were honest with me."

Madison licked his lips. He clearly had the number he needed to call memorized, because he dialed it without hesitation. He put the phone on speaker so that Tyrian, Robin, and Kieran could listen to the other side of the conversation, and they all waited in silence.

"Yes?" Fay answered after a few rings.

"It's Madison."

"Took you long enough."

Tyrian wanted to yell at her for almost killing Madison, but he couldn't ruin this. Madison only cared about his sister, and Tyrian wanted to get her back.

"I had to go to the hospital. I got burned badly."

"But you're with the pack now?"

That was all she cared about. Considering what Tyrian knew of her, he wasn't surprised. It was a miracle that Kieran and his brother were good men when their sister was so rotten.

"How's Katie?" Madison asked.

"The brat is fine. Tell me what you found out."

Madison's gaze flickered to Kieran, who nodded at him to continue.

"I don't know anything yet. Your brother found me in the building, and they took me to the hospital. He's keeping me locked up in a room until he can talk to me because he doesn't know if he can trust me."

"You won't get a lot of information locked up in a bedroom."

Madison pressed his lips together for a second. Tyrian had to resist the urge to reach for him and try to comfort him. Madison was strong. He could do this.

"I'll do everything I can to get out of here. I just need to convince Kieran to trust me." Madison looked at Kieran again as he said those words.

Kieran smiled and nodded, a silent sign that Madison was doing well. The approval seemed to please Madison, who gave a tiny nod back.

"Well, my brother trusts a bunch of vampires," Fay said, her voice dripping with disgust. "He'll have to trust you, since you grew up together."

Tyrian was surprised to hear that, even though Kieran and Madison seemed to be around the same age. Kieran hadn't known what was happening to Madison, though, so it was clear they hadn't been close.

"I'm sure I can convince him," Madison agreed.

Going along with this plan was the best thing they could do at the moment, but it would mean coming up with false information to give Fay while at the same time attempting to find their way to Katie. Fay might be a nasty person, but she wasn't stupid. She had to anticipate that Madison might try something, which meant she would keep Katie in a place where Madison couldn't get to her.

This wasn't going to be easy, but that had never stopped Tyrian. When he wanted to save someone, he did, no matter what he had to do.

And he desperately wanted to save Madison.

CHAPTER THREE

It had only been a few days, but Madison could already tell when something was wrong with Tyrian. It surprised him, yet at the same time, it didn't. He was fascinated by the vampire, and there wasn't much to do but watch him. Kieran had made sure Madison had books and a TV, and of course, he had the phone he was supposed to use to communicate with Fay, but he wasn't used to being stuck in one room.

He wasn't a prisoner, or at least, that was what everyone kept saying. Yet he hadn't left the room. It had become his, and he wasn't sure how he felt about that, and not just because the house was full of vampires.

Realizing that had made him uneasy at first. Tyrian had been honest with him and had explained that his entire family was there and shared the house, and while Madison trusted him not to hurt him, he wasn't sure about the others. He didn't think Meyer would do anything, but he didn't know the rest of the family, and it made him anxious.

Of course, there was little about this situation that *didn't* make him anxious.

He hadn't heard from Fay again, and he hadn't called her. Kieran and his brother and the people they trusted were coming up with false information Fay would be satisfied with. That was way above Madison's pay grade, but he'd be happy to pass on whatever they thought was appropriate. As long as Fay believed he was helping, she wouldn't hurt Katie, which was Madison's main goal.

He might be stuck in this bedroom, but it wasn't such a bad

thing. He'd never been allowed to watch TV or play around on the Internet whenever he wanted, so it was a treat. Having Tyrian spend so much time with him was, too, and he'd gotten to know the vampire.

Which wasn't helping with his stupid crush.

Tyrian might not have been the one who pulled Madison out of the fire, but Madison's heart didn't seem to have gotten that memo. It was set on Tyrian, and it raced wildly every time the vampire was in the bedroom. He was the one who usually brought food to Madison, and Madison had been surprised to find out that Tyrian cooked. Vampires didn't eat, so it didn't make sense, but it was just one more thing that fascinated Madison and made him want to ask hundreds of questions. So far, he'd kept his mouth under control.

He wasn't sure he could do so for much longer.

Tyrian had brought him dinner, and while he usually sat with him at the small desk he'd brought in the day after Madison had arrived, today he was standing by the window looking out. His back was tense, and he'd barely looked at Madison, which wasn't like him. He always fussed quite a bit, almost as if he cared about Madison.

Madison lowered his fork. "What's going on?"

Tyrian turned his attention to him. "Nothing. Is the food not good?"

Madison looked down at the pasta salad. It had cherry tomatoes and pesto, and he'd never put anything that tasted so good in his mouth before. "It's perfect. I can see something is bothering you, though, and it's making me worry."

"You have nothing to worry about."

Tyrian's answer was quick but didn't make Madison feel better. Clearly something had happened, and he needed to know what it was because of Katie.

Tyrian quickly came to stand next to Madison. He was careful not to touch him, but then, he seldom did. It was as if he was afraid to hurt Madison, and he wasn't wrong. His arms and hands still ached. Even though using the fork was hell, Madison refused to let anyone feed him, including Tyrian. He was used to doing everything on his own, and while he'd never been wounded like he was now, that didn't mean he was incapable of taking care of himself.

"I promise this has nothing to do with Katie," Tyrian said, looking Madison in the eyes.

Madison wanted to believe him. "What is it, then? You don't have to tell me if you're not comfortable, but I can see something's bothering you."

Tyrian hesitated. "I have a meeting."

That wasn't what Madison had expected. "Okay."

"It's not in pack territory. We're meeting a coven leader, and we have to go to him. Well, he's meeting us halfway, but it means Kieran and I need to go."

Madison still couldn't see what the problem was. "You don't want to travel with Kieran?"

"I have no problem with Kieran. It's you I'm worried about."

Madison blinked. He hadn't expected that and had no idea how to take it. Was Tyrian worried that Madison would try to run? Was that why he didn't want to leave him alone? Or was there something else that Madison wouldn't dare hope for?

His stupid crush had to be one-sided, dammit. If it wasn't, he'd never get out of it.

"I don't expect anyone to attack you or anything like that," Tyrian continued. "But I'm not sure I'm comfortable leaving you behind. You're still healing, and you don't always take that seriously."

That much was true. The first day, Tyrian insisted that he feed Madison and help him wash up. Madison had refused, and Tyrian has been grumpy about it since then. Madison understood where he was coming from. He was always tempted to do things for Katie because he loved her and wanted to be useful, but he'd often had to top himself. She needed to learn things on her own, and she was old enough to do so.

So was he. He thought maybe Tyrian understood that, but it was clear that the vampire was overprotective. From what little Meyer had told Madison, Tyrian was extremely caring. He enjoyed taking care of people, and it had been a while since he'd had anyone to do that for. Then Madison had entered the picture, and now Tyrian's instincts were out of control.

"Maybe it would be good for you to be away from me for a bit," Madison said.

Tyrian cocked his head. "How do you figure that?"

Madison looked down at his plate. "I enjoy spending time with you, and I feel we're becoming friends, but you've been spending almost every night with me."

Madison wasn't used to being awake during the night and sleeping during the day, but his routine was shifting. He didn't have anything to do but heal and eat, and he found himself spending the first part of the night talking to Tyrian. He usually fell asleep around one or two in the morning, and by the time he woke up, it was time for Tyrian to go to his room and rest for the day. He'd explained that the sun wouldn't hurt him and that he was old enough to be able to walk in it, but as a vampire with younger children, he was used to being awake during the night, and he wasn't planning to change that.

It was fine. Madison didn't mind being awake during the night, especially when he couldn't leave the room.

"I wouldn't be spending every night with you if I didn't enjoy it," Tyrian pointed out.

"I never said you didn't enjoy it. It's just that I'm sure you have better things to do, and now you have the opportunity to do them. Go to your meeting. It sounds important, and I'll

43

be fine here." Maybe Madison could read something. He tended to avoid social media because it sucked him in, and by the time he looked up again, two hours had passed and he'd done nothing productive, but it might be a good way to waste half an hour or so. If that failed, there was always the TV.

"I do have a few things to take care of," Tyrian said, but he still sounded hesitant.

"Then go do them, because you don't need to watch over me. I'm not a child."

"I never thought you were. All right. I'll go to my meeting, but I want you to know that you can call me for anything."

Madison grinned. "Even if I need my nose scratched?"

Tyrian laughed, and Madison loved that he could do that. Tyrian had been incredibly serious in the beginning, barely cracking a smile, but he was more relaxed now. He always smiled when Madison spoke, and Madison had made him laugh a few times. It made him wonder what Tyrian would sound like in bed, but he quickly pushed that thought away.

There was no future there. Even though Tyrian seemed to like him, Madison was sure it was only because he wanted to save him. The people he'd turned all had their own lives, so he didn't have to take care of them anymore.

But Madison was different. Madison needed him, and while he didn't like feeling like he depended on someone, he was going to take advantage of it for as long as he could.

Tyrian wasn't worried that something would happen to Madison or that he would be attacked. Madison was safe here, surrounded by Tyrian's family. Tyrian had already mentioned the meeting to Meyer and asked him to keep an eye on Madison, which for some reason, had amused Meyer greatly.

But he'd agreed, so Tyrian knew Madison would be all right while he, Kieran, and Merrick went to visit Merrick's coven leader. Tyrian had never met Harmon, but he was on their side, and it was important to coordinate with him. Hopefully, through him, more supernatural creatures would ally with the pack. The dragons were a danger to everyone in their community, not just Kieran's people, and people needed to understand that.

Tyrian had been excited about the meeting, but now, it filled him with dread. He didn't want to leave Madison, and he'd been tempted to mention to Kieran that he wished Madison could come with them.

He'd known better. Merrick was still extremely suspicious of Madison. No one blamed him, not even Madison himself, but there was no way he'd agree to have him come along. Besides, Madison still needed rest. He was healing, but it was slow going, which wasn't a surprise considering how extensive his wounds had been — and still were.

So Madison wasn't going anywhere. Tyrian needed to make his peace with that, especially because no one was going to hurt Madison while he wasn't there. He trusted the wolves and Meyer and the rest of the family even more.

So why was it so hard to step away? Even though Madison had just said he was fine with Tyrian leaving for a bit, Tyrian wanted to stick close. He gestured at Madison's plate instead of saying that out loud. "You should finish your meal."

Madison rolled his eyes, but he dug in with enthusiasm. Tyrian laughed at that. He'd always enjoyed cooking, but the fact that he didn't have to eat made it a bit boring, not to mention wasteful. He'd always cooked for the people he'd turned into vampires, but there was no one like that in his life at the moment. He supposed he could feed Arlen and Merrick, Mallory and Alpin's dragons, but sometimes, he wondered if Merrick was tempted to make *him* his next meal. Merrick was always grumpy except when Alpin was involved, and even then, it was dicey.

"Call me, whatever you need," Tyrian insisted.

"I'm not going to bother you when you have an important meeting. I'm sure you're leaving someone behind to keep an eye on me."

"Meyer will be here. I wasn't sure if you'd be comfortable having him in your private space, so I told him to stay out of the room, but you can invite him in."

Madison's smile was sweet. It made Tyrian want to lean forward and kiss him, and it was hard to resist the urge.

"Everything is set, then."

Tyrian supposed everything was. He checked his watch, noticed he was almost late, and once again resisted the urge to kiss Madison. "I have to go."

"Then go. I'll be here when you come back."

Tyrian quickly moved to the door. He closed it behind himself, but he didn't lock it. He never had, not even right after Madison had arrived. Madison wasn't going anywhere, and not because he was wounded. He wanted to be in pack territory. He wanted this place to be his home again and for his sister to be given back to him. The pack was his best bet when it came to that happening, and he knew it.

He found Meyer leaning against the wall in the hallway and nodded at him. Meyer nodded back, a smile playing on his lips.

"I'll keep an eye on your man. Don't worry," he promised.

Tyrian didn't even try to refute the fact that Madison was his man. "Thank you. I have my phone on me, so call if anything happens."

"Everything will be fine. The others are curious about Madison, but they won't bother him. I'll make sure he doesn't feel lonely."

"Why are they curious?"

"Because it's been a long time since anyone has caught your attention. You also look happier, which I'm not sure I understand, considering the situation."

Tyrian wasn't sure he felt happier, but something had settled in him after he'd met Madison. He hadn't allowed himself to explore that feeling yet, but he would eventually.

Just not right now.

He quickly left the house and headed to Kieran's home. The alpha was already standing by Merrick's car, talking to him as they waited. Both of them turned when they heard him, and while Merrick appeared annoyed, Kieran had a smile for Tyrian.

"How's Madison?" Kieran asked.

"He was eating dinner when I left. He's all right, healing and resting."

"Just like the doctor ordered. Has my sister contacted him yet?"

"Not that I'm aware of."

"I'm not sure if that's a good thing or a bad one," Kieran said with a sigh. "Ready to go?"

Tyrian nodded and climbed into the back seat. Kieran took the passenger seat in the front, while Merrick was driving. They were headed to meet the head of his coven, so it made sense, no matter how many times he grumbled that he was only half-vampire and that he didn't belong to a coven. As far as Tyrian was concerned, a vampire always belonged to their coven of origin. It was their first family in the vampire world, or at least, that was how things should be. He understood why Merrick wanted to stay away from vampires as much as he could, though. He'd heard part of his story, and while a vampire, Merrick was still a dragon. He was visibly more comfortable with shifters than with vampires, which was okay.

Thinking of Merrick made Tyrian wonder if a wolf shifter would be willing to be turned. He'd never tried turning anyone who wasn't human, and he wasn't about to start. There was no way Madison would agree to that. His sister was the most important person in his life, and he wouldn't do anything to jeopardize their relationship. She was only ten, but eventually she'd grow up and become an adult. She wouldn't need Madison as much as she did now, but Tyrian didn't know if he'd still be around when that happened.

And now really wasn't the right moment to think about that.

The drive passed quickly. Before he knew it, they were parking in front of a club. Tyrian had never been here, so he kept his eyes and ears open as they walked in.

The first thing he noticed was that the people moving on the dance floor and milling around were a mix of supernatural creatures. He'd expected the vampires, but not the shifters. He recognized a wolf, a lion, and even some kind of bird shifter as he walked past them. He could also smell earth and grass, which meant there was probably some kind of creature linked to nature around.

But the most overwhelming scent of all belonged to humans. They were unaware of what most of the people around them were, and as long as they were safe, they'd never know they'd partied and danced with people who weren't human.

Merrick appeared more relaxed, maybe because he used to own a club like this one before the clan had burned it down. He and Arlen were rebuilding, and while at first Tyrian had been surprised to learn that Merrick had a job that put him in contact with the public, he wasn't so much anymore. He walked tall and like this place belonged to him, cutting a path through the crowd. Everyone gave him a wide berth. They didn't seem afraid of him, but they were wary and knew he could hurt them.

It was a good thing for them that he didn't want to.

"There," Merrick said over the music as he pointed toward a corner of the club.

He led Kieran and Tyrian toward a more private area. Several tables were separated from the general area by partitions, and once they were allowed to walk through, Merrick made a beeline for one of the tables. A man was sitting there, bent over his phone, but he looked up when he heard them. His long brown hair was tied on the nape of his neck, and when he stood up, Tyrian could see he was tall.

"Welcome," Harmon said.

Madison hadn't been surprised when he'd heard Tyrian talk to someone outside of his door. Tyrian had been freaking out about leaving Madison on his own, and it hadn't been a surprise to find out he'd asked Meyer to spend time with him.

The other vampire had knocked almost immediately after Tyrian had left. Madison had finished eating, and they'd watched each other for a moment. It had been awkward, and it still was. It was clear Meyer wasn't used to spending time with strangers. Madison just had to look at how tense he was, sitting on the edge of the chair by the desk.

He'd told Madison he was here to keep him company, but he hadn't said anything so far. Madison didn't mind, but if Meyer was going to stay quiet, maybe it would be better for him to leave. Madison wasn't about to suggest it, though. Tyrian had given an order, and Meyer would follow it.

From what Madison had seen, it was obvious that every person Tyrian had turned into a vampire respected him immensely. They didn't have to follow his orders, but they did anyway. It made Madison feel better about ending up in Tyrian's hands, but he hadn't been too worried to begin with. Nothing could be worse than having to follow Fay.

Part of him hoped he could stay in Tyrian's life even after all of this was over, and if that was going to happen, he needed to be comfortable with Tyrian's family. Meyer was one of those people, so maybe Madison should make an effort.

He cleared his throat. "So you know pretty much everything about me. I don't know anything about you, though."

Meyer arched a brow. "What do you want to know?"

"I don't know. Whatever you're comfortable sharing with me, I guess."

Meyer stared. He was quiet so long that Madison was sure he wasn't going to answer, so he was surprised when the words came out of Meyer's mouth.

"I had a sister once, too," he said.

Madison blinked. "You did?" He hadn't missed the fact that Meyer was talking about her in the past tense. Since Meyer was a vampire, it wasn't a surprise, but it still had to hurt. "I'm sorry for your loss."

For some reason, the words made Meyer smile. "Thank you. She passed away a long time ago, but I miss her. She was the only person in my human family who knew what happened to me."

"She knew you were a vampire?"

Vampires, like shifters, kept their existence a secret. Humans tended to freak out over things different from them, especially things they didn't understand. No one knew how vampires survived on blood or how they could turn humans. No one knew how shifters could become animals, just that they could. It was as natural as breathing to them, and they didn't need to know the why or how behind it.

But humans weren't like that. They poked and prodded until they got their answers, and since they didn't like anyone who wasn't like them, it was a fair bet that they would have freaked out if they'd known about the supernatural world.

The secrecy was easier on shifters. They grew up in packs, which meant they always had someone. The same couldn't be said for vampires. Unless they were turned as part of a coven, they were on their own, and Madison could only imagine how lonely that was.

"She did. I knew she wouldn't freak out when I told her. She'd always loved reading and was fascinated by the stories of fairies and things like that. She loved me no matter what I was."

"She sounds like a good person."

"I couldn't have asked for a better sister, which is why I asked to turn her. She refused. She always did, no matter how angry I got at her or how much I begged. She told me that she was happy that Tyrian had turned me, because I would have died if he hadn't, but that this wasn't a life for her. She wanted to fall in love, have children, and grow old, and that's what she did."

"You gave her what she wanted even though you knew you'd lose her eventually."

Meyer nodded. "Wouldn't you do the same for your sister?"

"I'd do pretty much everything for her." Including agreeing to spy on the pack he'd always considered his home.

He was glad he didn't have to keep it a secret and that Kieran knew. If he'd lied to Kieran about why he was here, Katie wouldn't have had a home anymore. Madison still hoped the two of them would be able to move back with the pack permanently once this was over, so it was important to him to keep Kieran on his side. But if it had been necessary for him to lie and actually spy on Kieran, he would have done it.

For Katie.

He missed her like missing a limb. She'd been in his life for the past ten years, and he'd cared for her because no one else would, not even their father. Madison was in his early twenties when she was born, and he'd always felt more like her father than her brother. He'd been the one to raise her, and he'd kill for her if he had to.

He hoped he wouldn't need to do that.

"Katie is lucky to have you," Meyer said with a smile.

Madison found himself smiling back. He'd been wary of vampires before, and he still was, but he'd come to realize that just like shifters, vampires were extremely different from one another. There were good vampires, just like there were bad vampires.

But Tyrian and Meyer were good people. They might drink blood to survive, but they hadn't attacked Madison. If anything, they were taking care of him, and getting to know them had shown Madison that they were just like him. They had people they loved and for whom they would sacrifice anything. They had people who annoyed them and even people they hated. They had feelings and emotions, and they weren't the bloodthirsty monsters his father had always told him about.

That had just been another lie.

"And your sister was lucky to have you."

Meyer's smile widened. It exposed his fangs, but for the first time, Madison wasn't freaking out. So what if Meyer had fangs? Madison could turn into a freaking wolf.

"So Tyrian saved your life?" he asked. He was curious about Tyrian's family and how it had come to be.

"He did. He saved every member of our little family. Some of us were wounded, others sick. He took us all in and cared for us, and once he was sure there was nothing he could do to help us survive as humans, he gave us a choice."

Madison tried to imagine how that would feel. What would he do if he was on the brink of death and someone offered to turn him into a vampire?

The answer came to him right away. If it meant not having to leave Katie, he'd say yes to whatever was needed to keep him alive. He was sure Meyer had felt the same way, and probably the others, too. They'd all had a good reason to take what Tyrian was offering.

They wanted to live. That was what everyone always wanted, and it was stupid to be afraid of them just because of that. They couldn't change the fact that they were vampires, but they didn't have to.

"He likes you," Meyer continued.

Madison didn't know what to think of that. "Well, it looks like he likes pretty much everyone." There was no way Tyrian felt any kind of special emotion when it came to Madison.

"He does tend to like a lot of people. You're special, though."

"Because I'm wounded, and he wants to help me." Madison looked down at his hands. They were the only reason Tyrian was sticking around. Once Madison was better, he'd have better things to focus on, and Madison wouldn't see him anymore.

"Maybe. He certainly has a protective streak big enough to want to keep an eye on you. I wouldn't swear on the fact that it's the only reason he's spending time with you, though."

Madison wanted to believe Meyer, but what other reason could there be?

"I think we should use him," Merrick declared, looking around the table defiantly.

Tyrian didn't miss the way he avoided looking at him. There was no doubt Merrick knew he'd be opposed to that plan.

He was. No matter how Merrick felt about him, Tyrian wasn't putting Madison in danger. "He's wounded and already agreed to help us," he pointed out.

"That's not enough. He set fire to that building."

Tyrian squared his shoulders and glared at Merrick. "He

didn't, and you'd know that if you'd given him a chance to explain."

Merrick snorted. "You believe him?"

"I do. I've been spending time with him and talking to him, and he's not the kind of person who would lie about something like that."

"You're thinking with your dick instead of your brain."

Kieran cleared his throat. "I'm with Tyrian on this one. I don't believe Madison wanted to hurt anyone, and I think he's telling the truth when he says he didn't set the fire. He went along with this for his sister, and he didn't know what Fay was planning until he was knocked out."

"Yet he saw what was happening. How is that possible if he was knocked out?" Merrick insisted.

"Fay wanted us to take him in," Tyrian said as calmly as he could. "She thought we'd do it more easily if he was wounded, and she wasn't wrong. Even though we were suspicious of him, he was hurt, and we stepped in to help. That was before we knew what had happened to him, but we already suspected that he might be a spy. She wanted to be sure he'd be welcomed, and that's what happened. She got what she wanted."

"A spy in the pack," Merrick said, sounding smug.

"A false spy. Madison told us why he's there, remember? He said that Fay wanted him to spy on us and explained the situation even though it would have been safer for him not to."

"He's playing us," Merrick insisted.

Tyrian was done arguing with him. "He's putting his sister's life in danger," he snapped. "He knew he would, yet he told us everything anyway. Do you have any idea what would happen to her if Fay were to find out about this? She doesn't care that Katie is only ten. She's using her as leverage, and as long as Madison goes along with what she wants, she won't hurt her, but can we be sure of that? Can't you see the kind of sacrifice Madison was ready to make?"

"I agree we need to do something," Kieran interjected.

Tyrian was grateful for the interruption. He felt like he could continue yelling at Merrick for hours, and Merrick still wouldn't understand his point of view. The man was as stubborn as they came, which wasn't a surprise, considering he and Alpin were together. Alpin needed someone strong to stand up to him, and he'd found it in Merrick.

But Merrick was a pain in Tyrian's ass now, and he wished he could kick him to the curb and out of this meeting.

"I doubt your sister will stop, even if she gets what she wants," Harmon said. "She doesn't strike me as someone who cares about how many people she has to hurt to get what she wants."

"She feels that the pack should have been hers, and you're right. Once she gets the pack back, she'll want to expand. If she still has the dragons on her side when that happens, it could bring down a good portion of the supernatural community."

Tyrian didn't like that Kieran was talking as if that was going to happen. They were working hard to make sure it didn't, and especially now that Madison was in the picture, Tyrian would do what he could to protect the pack. It was home to two of his sons and Madison, and there was nothing more important to Tyrian than family.

"That means we need to find allies."

Tyrian agreed. Luckily, he was fairly old, which meant he'd met his fair share of supernatural creatures over the decades. "I've already contacted several people. Some agreed to help, while others have decided to stay back and see how things go first."

Merrick snorted. "You mean they decided to see if Fay kills us before they do anything."

Tyrian gritted his teeth. He told himself that Merrick was worried for his family and Alpin and that it was natural. His reaction was to attack and be grumpy, but it wasn't something he could help.

"Possibly," Tyrian agreed. "I never expected everyone to come running when I asked them for help, but a good number of people have agreed to stand by our side. Unfortunately, not everyone is in the area."

"I might be able to help with that," Harmon said. "I know people, too, and most of them live around here." He kept peeking at Merrick as if he expected him to explode.

Tyrian wouldn't have minded that too much at the moment.

"I've already reached out to other alphas," Kieran added. "I think this is the only thing we can do. We don't know where Fay is, and there's no way we can take on the clan head-on."

"I still think Madison knows where Fay and the others are," Merrick grumbled.

Madison had told them where they'd been staying, but when Kieran had sent people, the place was empty. No one had been surprised. Fay would have been stupid not to move her people often, and she'd known there was a chance that Madison would betray her. She hadn't been wrong, but hopefully, she didn't know it.

They had to be in town somewhere, close enough to attack the pack, but that was all anyone was sure of. Not knowing where his sister was scared Madison because he felt that there was nothing he could do for her. He might be right, but Tyrian had promised he'd do what he could to get Katie back, and he hadn't been lying.

Over just a few days, he'd come to care for Madison a great deal. He didn't understand why, but he suspected that a good part of it was his protective instinct. Another part was that

Madison was adorable and gentle, a nice person who'd found himself in the worst situation. He was doing what he could with what he had and desperately trying to save his sister, and Tyrian could understand that.

The main reason he'd started turning people who were dying was that he hadn't had anyone. He'd lost his entire family decades before turning his first vampire, and the loneliness had gotten to him. He'd yearned for a new family. Now, he had it.

But he was still missing something. He was missing what Mallory and Alpin had found, a love so big that it would change his life. He didn't know if Madison could be that love, but he was interested in the shifter. That was enough for him to do what he could to help Madison and his sister, but he'd never demand anything in exchange.

He was pretty sure that Madison was as interested in him as he was in Madison, and maybe it was worth exploring. He trusted that Madison wasn't double-crossing them, and he didn't care how Merrick felt or what he believed, just about what he and Madison wanted.

Hopefully, it was the same thing.

It didn't matter that Tyrian's feelings had developed over only a few days. In the decades he'd lived, he'd learned to follow his instincts, and he would this time, too. He trusted Madison. Madison was on their side. That was all there was to it. Tyrian wasn't willing to use him. Hopefully, Kieran felt the same way.

Tyrian wouldn't hesitate to take Madison away if he had to.

He hoped it wouldn't come to that. He didn't want to disappoint the alpha, especially with two of his sons living with the pack. Besides, Kieran was a good person. Even if he were to decide to use Madison, he'd only do it because he felt he didn't have a choice. That meant that Tyrian had to show him there was a choice and devise alternate plans that would satisfy Kieran and Merrick.

It wouldn't be easy, but Tyrian believed that the only way to face Fay and the clan was to come up with their own allies. They had one in Harmon, and hopefully they could find many others.

And once they did, the war would begin. They'd have to fight to survive, and Tyrian had no doubt they'd lose people. He didn't want to live with regret, and he certainly didn't want to die with regrets. That meant giving a chance to whatever was growing between him and Madison.

And he was ready to do just that.

CHAPTER FOUR

"You've been there for a week. This is all you have?"

Madison sucked in a breath. He'd given Fay everything Kieran had come up with, but they had to be careful with the amount of information he passed on. She'd know something was up if he gave her too much since he'd told her he was locked in a bedroom. He had to find a balance, but it wasn't easy. Fay didn't expect more, but she wanted it, and she didn't seem to care that it would be impossible if Madison really was locked up.

Besides, he kind of was. Everyone kept telling him he wasn't a prisoner, but he hadn't been allowed to leave the bedroom. They'd told him it was because he was still healing and needed rest, but Madison knew it was because they didn't trust him. They still thought he was working for Fay and that he'd run back to her if he had the opportunity. They didn't understand that Madison would rather die than do that. The only reason he would ever go back was Katie, but he wouldn't get her unless he gave Fay something massive.

Either way, he felt like he was losing.

"I'm doing my best. They still have me locked up, so I've been sneaking out the window and listening in when possible. You knew they wouldn't trust me right away."

"Do they still think you set fire to the building?"

"They suspect I did. It's where they found me, after all."

"Fine. Tell them it was me so they start trusting you. You need to get out of that room."

"I doubt they'd believe me. They'd probably think I'm

59

trying to convince them to let me out, and they wouldn't be wrong."

Madison understood why she was angry. She expected him to give her the key to the pack, but instead, the only information he was passing on was how the pack was dealing with the fire, some of the people Kieran was talking to, and his plans when it came to Fay. Madison didn't know much about the truth behind the lies Kieran had asked him to pass on, but even if he did, he wouldn't tell Fay. Kieran was his only chance to get Katie back and for them to have a happy future.

As long as Fay didn't hurt her.

"I sent you there for a reason," Fay said. "If you're not useful to me and our new pack, you know what's going to happen."

Madison swallowed and looked at Tyrian. He was always present when Madison talked to Fay, and Madison was grateful. He didn't know what he would have done if he'd had to face this alone or even with a different person. Tyrian was always reassuring, no matter what Fay said. It was what Madison needed, but right now, Madison wasn't sure it was enough.

"I'll do better," he promised.

"You should if you don't want something to happen to your sister."

Madison didn't know what to say. He wasn't surprised Fay was threatening Katie, but what could he do beyond begging her not to hurt his sister? He couldn't betray the pack. If he did, he'd hurt good people and take away the only chance Katie had to come home.

But if he didn't betray them, Katie might get hurt, or worse. How was Madison supposed to make a choice? How was he supposed to choose between his sister and the only people who could save her?

A hand landed on his shoulder. He was startled, but that was because he hadn't expected it. Tyrian had kept his distance until now, maybe because he was afraid to hurt Madison or because he knew it would be better. He might have realized Madison had a stupid crush on him, which wasn't what Madison wanted, but he supposed he'd have to deal with it just like he was dealing with everything else. Right now, it was the least of his problems.

Tyrian squeezed, and that was enough to reassure Madison. They'd talked about Fay and Katie, and Tyrian had pointed out that Fay wouldn't hurt Katie. If she did, she'd lose the only pawn she was using to control Madison. She'd known he'd do anything to save his sister, but also that no one cared about him, which made him the perfect person to send to possibly die in a fire or to be killed by their old pack.

But Fay hadn't expected Madison to be honest with Kieran. She hadn't expected him to find allies, and to be honest, neither had he. He was still confused about why everyone, including Kieran, was so nice to him. He wouldn't betray their trust, but he prayed to whatever god was listening that his sister wouldn't pay for that.

"I'll do better," he promised in a whisper.

"See that you do. My patience has its limits."

She hung up. Madison lowered the phone and stared at the screen for a moment, but when it turned dark, he couldn't avoid the confrontation with Tyrian anymore.

"She says she's going to hurt Katie," he whispered.

Tyrian squeezed Madison's shoulder again before letting go. "She won't. Katie is the only reason you're doing this. She won't risk losing what she has over you, especially not when you haven't given her anything useful yet."

"She's going to run out of patience eventually." And that was what scared Madison the most. Fay wanted him to spy on the pack, but her end goal was to take the pack back and become the alpha. That wouldn't happen if she waited for Madison to hand over the right information without doing anything more. She wasn't exactly impulsive, but she was desperate to show the people who'd followed her and the dragon clan that she could do this.

Madison was always worried about the fact that Fay might have already hurt Katie. He'd asked to talk to his sister as soon as Fay had answered, but she'd refused. She'd said she wasn't with Katie at the moment, and while that might be true, Madison was terrified that Fay had hurt her. As long as she refused to let him talk to her, he couldn't be sure Katie was even alive, and the thought that she might not be made him panic.

Tyrian crouched in front of Madison. "Breathe," he ordered. "She doesn't have a reason to hurt your sister."

"What if she's already killed her?" Madison whispered.

"I don't think she has. She's on the run and hiding, and the last thing she needs is a dead body to get rid of. Besides, since Katie's the only reason you're doing this, she has to know that she can use your sister to force you into other things. It would be stupid to have killed your sister, and while I don't like Fay, I don't think she's stupid."

Madison had to agree. Fay wasn't a good person, but that didn't make her an idiot. It also didn't make her smart, and sometimes, she *was* impulsive. Hopefully, that would play in Kieran's favor, but there was no way to know anything for sure.

Madison hated that he was stuck in this bedroom. He wanted to do more, even though he didn't know what that more was.

He threw the phone onto the bed and got up. He was healing, and his legs didn't hurt anymore. They hadn't been burned, but he'd been wounded by whatever had fallen on top of him during the fire. They were fine now, and his arms and hands were getting there. He always avoided looking down at them when the doctor checked the skin, but eventually, he would have to. The fact that he was horribly burned and that he'd have scars didn't matter. He had bigger things to focus on.

Everyone did.

Fay had been blitz-attacking pack businesses in town and pack members. She hadn't set fire to all the buildings, but people were getting hurt and losing their livelihoods, and it didn't sit well with Madison. It made him feel guilty, even though he had nothing to do with the attacks. He wanted to do more to protect the pack and to get Katie back, but what?

He turned to Tyrian, who'd gotten to his feet. "I need to do more."

"You're already doing more than enough." Tyrian didn't hesitate when he answered. He probably truly believed that.

Madison shook his head. "I feel useless here. I keep passing information, but Fay isn't wrong. I won't get anything she needs unless Kieran lets me out, and I'm sure she has people watching me. Maybe we can give her more if I'm allowed out of this bedroom. I can tell her that Kieran is starting to trust me but still keeps an eye on me. That would explain why you're always with me."

Tyrian stared for a moment. Madison expected him to say no and to tell him to get back to bed, even though he didn't need to.

But instead, Tyrian nodded. "What did you have in mind?"

Tyrian didn't particularly want Madison to leave his bedroom—he was afraid Madison would get hurt, and it wasn't his place to feel that way. There was nothing between them, and nothing could happen unless Madison was free. It wouldn't be right.

He didn't have permission from Kieran to let Madison out, but he didn't think that would be a problem. It wasn't like Madison was asking to be let in on meetings with the pack allies. He just wanted to do something and to be able to give Fay what she wanted to keep his sister safe. It was worth it, which was the only reason Tyrian was considering it.

Madison raked a hand through his hair. He didn't wince, which was a sign that his hand didn't hurt as much as it had. It was good to see, but something in Tyrian didn't want that to be the case. As long as Madison was still in pain, Tyrian could keep him safe here. Now that he'd almost healed, Tyrian would have to let him go. Madison would probably be in danger, and Tyrian wasn't sure how he'd deal with that.

But he was about to find out.

"I don't know," Madison admitted. "I just want to do more, you know? And it's not just because I hope that I'll be able to give Fay more and that she'll be satisfied. I hate that I'm stuck here, but even more, I hate that the pack believes I'm a traitor. The only reason I left was Katie, and I'm doing everything I can to save her while at the same time working to find her a new home. I can't do any of that if I'm stuck here."

Madison was understandably frustrated. Tyrian wanted to reassure him that he'd help, but he wasn't sure that was what Madison was looking for. Like always, the only thing on his mind was his sister. It was sweet and something Tyrian respected, and he knew he wasn't the only one. As it was, Merrick was the only one who still didn't trust Madison. It probably wouldn't be hard to convince Kieran to allow Madison to leave the bedroom. He decided it was time to do just that.

Madison was on the right side, on *their* side. It wasn't right to keep him prisoner.

"Let me call Kieran," he told Madison. "He'll probably be able to find you something to do. That means you'll have to deal with other pack members, though. Are you ready for that?"

"As long as they don't try to hurt me, I don't care what they think of me. I can't be the only one here who's ready to do anything for someone they love."

Tyrian knew he wasn't, but when people were angry, it wasn't always easy to see the truth that was in front of them. Besides, people might understand why Madison would betray the pack, but his betrayal would put them in danger along with the people they loved. Doing everything they could to protect them might include keeping Madison at arm's length.

Tyrian supposed they were about to find out how the pack would react to him being back. Letting Madison out was right, but that didn't mean Tyrian would abandon him. He didn't even care if Kieran told him to find something else to do. Tyrian's place was by Madison's side, and that was where he would be.

He took his phone out and quickly dialed Kieran's number. He had it memorized, which wasn't surprising. They kept in contact through phone calls and messages because Kieran had been spending a lot of time in town, taking care of the businesses and people that were attacked. He wasn't sure how to deal with his sister, and unfortunately, Tyrian didn't know, either. He was lost because he'd never had to deal with anything like this.

"Please tell me there isn't another problem I have to deal with," Kieran begged when he answered.

Tyrian smiled. "I don't know if I'd call it a problem. Madison is asking me to be allowed out of his bedroom. He wants to help."

"Help how?"

"He doesn't know, and I don't think he cares. He just had a phone call with your sister, and she threatened Katie again. She wasn't happy that he couldn't give her more, but he pointed out that he couldn't give her anything else until he was allowed out of the bedroom. I think it would be a good idea to do just that. If she has more spies, and I don't doubt she does, they'll see Madison, so when he gives her more false information, she'll believe him more readily. Giving her false information is all good and well, but it won't help us if we can't use it to our advantage."

"I don't like keeping him in that bedroom, anyway. But you know Merrick isn't going to be happy."

"I'll ask Alpin to deal with him."

Kieran chuckled. "Better him than me. Honestly, I'm not sure what those two see in each other, but I'm glad they're together. I'm pretty sure Merrick's head would've exploded a few times if it weren't for Alpin."

Tyrian had been surprised by the kind of man Alpin had chosen, but it was clear to everyone that they were good for each other. They complemented each other's personalities, and it was something both of them sorely needed.

"All right," Kieran said. "You can let him out."

"What should I have him do?"

"Well, with all the buildings Fay destroyed and the broken windows and stuff, there's a lot of cleaning to do. I know he was badly wounded, but would he feel okay helping with the cleanup?"

Tyrian wanted to say no, but instead, he turned to Madison. "Let me ask." He lowered his phone. "Kieran wants to know if you'd be okay with helping to clean up the businesses Fay's been attacking."

Even though Tyrian was offering hard work, Madison's eyes lit up and he nodded. "I can do whatever Kieran needs me to do. Besides, if Fay's people see me cleaning up, they might think I've been forced to do it. It will help us with her."

Tyrian wasn't sure about that, but it was him against Kieran and Madison. Besides, Madison was an adult and could make his own decisions. He'd decided to come here and spy on the pack, and he could decide to help with the cleanup.

"He's in," he told Kieran.

"Good. I want to trust him, Tyrian. I believe that he only agreed with Fay's plan to save his sister, and I'd do anything to save my brother or Robin. I want to help him, but I don't know how."

"We'll find a way." If Tyrian had to, he'd go out there on his own and rescue Katie by himself. He didn't know where she was yet, but he could find out, and Madison would be free when he did.

But first, they had to focus on the pack. As long as Fay was targeting them, no one in the pack would be safe, and that included Katie.

Tyrian hung up, and for a moment, he and Madison stared at each other. Then Madison grinned. "He says I can go, then?"

Madison was so beautiful that it made Tyrian's heart ache. He wanted to reach out, but he didn't want to push Madison into something he wasn't ready for. He hadn't wanted to try anything while Madison was a prisoner, but he wasn't anymore. Maybe later, Tyrian could finally take a step toward what he wanted.

But first, Madison needed to taste his freedom.

"You can help with the cleanup. He's sending me the address of the place he wants us to help at, so we can start heading out."

Madison was almost bouncing on his feet as he followed Tyrian out of the bedroom. The house was silent because everyone was helping protect the pack and clean the businesses that had been attacked. They were alone, but they wouldn't be for long.

It was time for Madison to rejoin the pack and take his place here. He was eager to do just that, but Tyrian was worried, and not just about Fay. This wouldn't be easy for Madison, and Tyrian didn't want his heart to break any more than it already had.

Madison knew this wouldn't be easy, and not just because they'd be cleaning the aftermath of a fire.

The pack didn't trust him. He didn't blame them, since he'd followed Fay when she left. Most of the pack didn't know him well, so they wouldn't be aware of the fact that he'd sacrifice anything to save his sister. Madison hadn't had a choice when their father took her away. The only way to keep Katie safe had been to follow, no matter how little he wanted it.

The pack members were wary. He'd expected them to be, but he'd hoped that at least a few would talk to him. Instead, they were giving him a wide berth, and while he was finally out of the bedroom, he felt like he was still completely alone.

Well, not completely. Tyrian stuck close by, picking up a few things and setting them aside while peeking at Madison every few minutes. Madison could see he wasn't cleaning much, but rather that he was hovering there to keep an eye on Madison. Madison wanted to believe it was because Tyrian didn't like the way the others were treating him and not because he didn't trust him, but how was he supposed to know? He was a traitor, after all. No one trusted him except possibly Tyrian, but he was afraid to ask. He didn't want to know if Tyrian didn't trust him.

But he had what he'd wanted. He'd been allowed to help, and even though his arms and hands ached, he wasn't about to stop. The pain didn't matter when he was helping the pack.

"Hey," someone said.

Madison looked around, wondering who Ollis was talking to. He was alone in the corner of the flower shop, trying to decide what to do with the burned and broken pots that had contained plants. Everyone else was at the front, picking up glass and boarding up the broken window.

But since Madison was alone except for Tyrian and Ollis, it meant Ollis was talking to him. Madison didn't know why. They'd never been friends, even though they were the same age. Well, Ollis was a few years younger, but that often didn't mean much in the pack.

"Hey," Madison said tentatively.

Ollis grinned. "It's good to finally see you out of that house. I know you were hurt."

Madison raised his hands. He was wearing gloves, but his arms were exposed. He wasn't ashamed of what had happened to him or of the scars, even though he wished they weren't there.

Ollis grimaced. "That has to hurt. Are you sure you should be here?"

"Yeah. I'd had enough of being stuck in that room."

"I can understand that. It's good to see you out and about, although I bet you wish you didn't have to clean up all of this."

"I wish there wasn't a reason for me to have to clean it up," Madison agreed.

The only reason he had to be here was that Fay had also set fire to the flower shop. The sight of so much destruction made him want to go to her and do something, but what? He didn't even know where she was. If he did, he could have gone and grabbed Katie.

The sound of people muttering made Madison turn. The others were staring at him, and even though they quickly looked away, there was no ignoring it.

Ollis snorted. "Ignore them. They're gossiping about you, but they don't know anything."

"I'm pretty sure they know enough."

"They think they know stuff, but no one does except for you, Kieran, and a few others. You don't have to tell me anything if you don't want to, but I just wanted to say that it was good to see you."

Madison had expected the other pack members not to trust him and to keep a wide berth. He wasn't sure why Ollis was behaving differently, but he was glad. They might not have been friends before, but that didn't mean they couldn't be now. Ollis could be talking to him out of pity, but right now, Madison was more than happy to have pity. Maybe if people pitied him, they'd be more open to welcoming him back into the pack.

"Why don't we take a break?" Ollis suggested.

Madison glanced at the others, but they weren't looking at him anymore. A few were still picking up glass debris, but several had sat down and were drinking water. He was thirsty, too, but he felt like if he rested, he'd be useless again. "I'm fine."

"Take a break," Tyrian ordered.

Ollis winked. "See. Even your bodyguard wants you to take a break."

"He's not my bodyguard," Madison muttered.

Ollis winked. "What is he, then? Your boyfriend? Because he's guarding your body like no one's business."

Madison felt his cheeks flush. He peeked at Tyrian, who he was sure had heard what Ollis had said. A smile played on his lips, but he was staring at the group of people on the other side of the store.

Madison carefully moved closer to Ollis. Ollis hopped up to sit on the counter, which had survived the fire. It was dirty, but then everything and everyone in the store was. The counter seemed sturdy enough, so Madison might as well, too.

Madison moved to do just that when Ollis patted the space next to him. The problem was that he couldn't put a lot of weight on his hands and arms, so it was tricky, at least until Tyrian stepped in. He didn't tell Madison not to sit there. Instead, he grabbed Madison's hips and hauled him up, setting him on the counter as if he were a child.

Madison's cheeks were on fire. Tyrian smiled gently, and while Madison knew he'd done it so he wouldn't hurt himself again, he couldn't help but read more into it.

Apparently, he wasn't the only one. As soon as Tyrian had stepped away, Ollis knocked his shoulder against Madison's.

"Your boyfriend, then?" Ollis gently pushed.

Madison shook his head. "It's not like that. I don't know why, but he's decided he needs to keep me safe, and that's all."

"And why do you think he decided to keep you safe? Kieran didn't order him to do so, did he?"

"Not as far as I'm aware."

"Then maybe he wants to keep you safe because he likes you."

Madison looked at Tyrian. He was close by, but far enough that he couldn't hear what they were saying. He'd be able to step in if anything happened to Madison, but he was giving Madison and Ollis privacy to talk, and Madison was glad for that. The problem was that he also wanted Tyrian close enough to touch him, which was the last thing he should do, considering how filthy he was. Besides, things were confusing and complicated enough. Madison didn't need to add to it.

Right?

"Even if he does like me, I don't think it's like a boyfriend," he murmured.

"I don't see why not. I mean, he's been watching you the entire time. Every time you move, he's there, making sure you're okay and that no one's bothering you. It's pretty clear he likes you, and I don't think it's in a friendly manner. A friend wouldn't hover that way."

Madison wanted to believe Ollis. "You think so?"

"Pretty much. I guess that the question here is whether or not you like him, too. I mean, I don't see what you wouldn't like. He's fucking hot, and the few times I've talked to him, he seemed like a good person."

"He is." Madison couldn't have hoped for a better person to shadow him.

"Then what is it? Is it because he's a vampire?"

Madison shook his head. His hesitation had nothing to do with that—it had everything to do with the fear of rejection. That wasn't the only thing. "You know what I did," he told Ollis without looking at him. "You know who I am. I'm a traitor, and it wouldn't be fair to put all of that on his shoulders. Besides, we've only known each other for a week or so. I'm sure he's hovering because he wants to make sure I don't hurt myself."

"I don't think you're a traitor."

Madison blinked and looked at Ollis. "I left, then came back." He didn't tell Ollis that Fay had sent him to spy on the pack. He couldn't bring himself to.

"Yeah, but I guess I would have done the same if I'd been in your place. Your family left, right? If you hadn't gone with them, you'd have been here on your own. Considering how these guys are treating you, I don't blame you for wanting to leave them behind."

Madison hadn't expected to find someone who would understand him beyond Tyrian, and he liked that Ollis was giving him a chance.

But he couldn't stop thinking about what Ollis had said. Could he really have a chance with Tyrian? Or were he and Ollis seeing what they wanted to see?

Tyrian couldn't hear most of Madison's conversation with

Ollis, but he didn't need to in order to know they were talking about him. He could feel them watching him, and every time he peeked back, it was to find Madison staring.

What was Ollis saying? That he'd noticed how much Tyrian had been staring at Madison? He wouldn't be wrong, because Tyrian couldn't keep his eyes off Madison, no matter what situation they were in.

Tyrian was curious, but Madison deserved his privacy, especially when he was with a friend. That was why even when the break was over and everyone started cleaning up again, Tyrian stayed away and gave the two space. Madison needed friends, and Ollis seemed to want to be that to him. It could only be a good thing.

When it was time to head back home, Ollis and Madison seemed to have become fast friends. They made plans to see each other the next day, but Madison was exhausted, and as Tyrian guided him toward the car with a hand on his back, he berated himself for not having stopped him sooner. He should have, but Madison had been so happy to be helpful and to talk to someone who wasn't Tyrian or Meyer that Tyrian hadn't had it in him to disappoint him.

"You did too much," he murmured as he opened the passenger seat door.

"Possibly," Madison agreed, surprising Tyrian.

He'd expected Madison to insist that he was fine and that he could do this again tomorrow. Maybe he could, but it wouldn't be good for him to work too hard when he was still hurt.

"Are you okay?" Madison asked.

Tyrian frowned, wondering why he was asking. "Why shouldn't I be?"

"Well, I didn't think about it when we left the house, but it was still the middle of the day."

They'd spent the afternoon at the flower shop with the

others, but now it was dark. Tyrian felt better, but even during the afternoon, he'd been fine. "I stayed inside as long as the sun was up," he explained. "I'm fine. I don't want you to worry about me because there's no reason for you to."

"I don't know about that. I mean, you're a vampire. You shouldn't be out and about in the sun."

"It's not the most comfortable thing, but it's not going to kill me. It's just annoying." And painful when he stayed too long in the sun and got sunburned, but that wasn't the case today, and he didn't want Madison to worry about something that hadn't happened.

As soon as Madison was in the passenger seat, Tyrian closed the door and rushed to the other side. When he climbed in, it was to see that Madison had pressed his forehead against the window. His eyes were closed, but Tyrian didn't think he was asleep. Still, he left him to his thoughts and started to drive back home.

Both of them were silent until they reached the house. There were people in now, but Tyrian and Madison avoided them. Tyrian suspected that Madison was too nervous to want to meet them, but eventually, he would have to. He wasn't a prisoner anymore, meaning he could leave his bedroom and explore the house. Maybe Tyrian should talk to the others first, though. They were curious about Madison, but having everyone's attention could be overwhelming.

He paused at Madison's door. "You should take a shower. I'm going to go downstairs and get you something to eat."

Madison nodded, but at the same time, he reached for Tyrian.

Tyrian immediately stilled, wondering what was happening.

Madison stared at the floor. "Look, I know now isn't the right moment to ask this, but I'm tired. I just want to know where we stand," Madison said.

His cheeks were red, and Tyrian had to resist the urge to reach for him. "What are you talking about?" he asked gently.

Madison finally looked up. He was biting his lower lip and looked like he wished he could be anywhere but here, but it wasn't enough to stop him. Madison was brave, and not only when it came to saving his sister.

"I guess I just want to know what's going on between us. Initially, I thought you were just keeping an eye on me because you didn't trust me. You've been spending most of your time with me, though, and it feels like a lot."

Tyrian told himself not to be hurt by those words. It was normal for Madison to want some space, especially from someone he barely knew and a vampire he didn't trust. "I'll ask Meyer to bring the food, then," he said stiffly.

Madison shook his head. "That's not what I was saying. I *like* spending time with you. I feel safe with you, and I guess I like you. But I don't understand what you're getting out of this. I'm just me, and I'm a traitor to boot. You could have so much better." His cheeks flushed harder. "Not that I'm saying you're interested in me in any way. It's just something Ollis said, but I'm sure he was wrong."

Tyrian understood now. Madison was asking him what was growing between them, and Tyrian was glad he'd noticed there was something. He'd been ready to give Madison as much space as he needed, but Madison was the one bringing this up. Surely that meant he wanted an honest answer.

Finally.

Tyrian reached for Madison's cheek. Madison's eyes went wide when Tyrian cupped it, but he didn't step away, not even when Tyrian leaned closer. Tyrian kissed Madison's cheek, then his forehead. "I've been hanging around so much because I didn't trust anyone else to keep you safe," Tyrian whispered. "And because I didn't trust anyone else to take care of you. I wasn't going to say anything until you were more settled, but I want you, Madison."

"I'm a traitor," Madison whispered.

"We both know that's not true. You're not a traitor. You're a worried brother. You're a man who was brave enough to do whatever was needed to keep his sister safe. I know all of you, Madison, and I can't think of a better man to fall in love with."

Maybe it was too much, but that was how Tyrian felt. He didn't want to overwhelm Madison, but he'd just told him he was falling in love with him. Could anything overwhelm him more than he already had?

So Tyrian closed the distance between them and pressed their lips together. Madison gasped, but he didn't push Tyrian away. Instead, he grabbed his shoulders and pulled him close, and Tyrian went because that was what he'd wanted to do since day one.

Madison felt perfect in Tyrian's arms. They were both covered in dirt and smelled of the fire, but Tyrian didn't care, and it was clear Madison didn't, either.

Tyrian had expected Madison to be hesitant and shy as they kissed, but the opposite was true. Madison always managed to surprise him, and he loved that. He might have been the one who took the first step and kissed Madison, but now Madison was pushing against him, devouring his mouth as if he could never get enough of it. Madison was everything Tyrian could have wanted and more, and Tyrian never wanted to let him go.

"You're so good to me," Madison whispered against Tyrian's lips.

"You deserve someone to be good to you. You deserve everything you want," Tyrian told him.

"I don't know if that's true, but I want this. I want something good in my life, something I don't have to fight for. I want *you*."

"And I'm yours for the taking."

Madison looked like he didn't quite believe that, but that was okay. They would have time once the mess with Fay was over and hopefully even before then. Tyrian was going to show Madison how much he cared about him, and if he needed Tyrian to do so more than once, that was what Tyrian would do. He wasn't letting Madison go now that he had him.

And it didn't matter that Madison didn't seem to believe there could truly be something between them. Madison was understandably wary, and it was a complicated situation, but Tyrian liked complicated.

And Madison.

Chapter Five

M adison had no idea how to behave, but that seemed to be normal for him these days. He didn't like feeling lost, but there was nothing he could do about it when he'd never been in this kind of situation.

Meeting the family.

He'd never met a partner's family, mostly because he'd never had a partner. He'd had boyfriends, but he'd had to keep them secret because of his father. He'd always chosen humans for that reason, and while he'd felt guilty, it had been just one more secret to keep. None of them had been serious relationships, anyway.

But the relationship with Tyrian was.

Madison had what he'd always wanted, but he still wasn't entirely sure where they stood. Tyrian had taken to them being together like it was natural. That day after the cleaning up of the flower shop, he'd brought Madison something to eat, and they'd cuddled on his bed until Madison had fallen asleep. He'd woken up late the next morning, and Tyrian was still next to him.

And since then, they'd been attached at the hip. Tyrian was always there, ready to help and protect him, and Madison loved it. No one had ever been there for him the way Tyrian was, and it made him feel cherished. He was pretty sure that some people would have felt it was too much and overwhelming, but not Madison. He wanted to lose himself in Tyrian and forget about all the bad things happening in the world. It wasn't realistic, but dreams didn't need to be.

But with their new relationship came Tyrian's family. He hadn't forced Madison into anything, but Madison felt like he needed to meet Tyrian's people. It was the least he could do, especially since he lived in the same house as they did. He already knew Meyer, but he was only one of them.

There were plenty of others.

Madison hadn't realized there were so many of them. He'd heard them move around the house, but from what he'd gathered, most of them were busy. That wasn't surprising, because everyone in the pack seemed to be busy, what with Fay, the businesses they needed to clean up and start rebuilding, and the dragon clan. But now they were all there, surrounding Madison, and he didn't know what to do.

Tyrian leaned closer and pressed a kiss to Madison's temple. "Relax. They're not going to eat you."

Madison bit his lower lip so he wouldn't laugh. "I'm aware of that."

He'd been wary, but he wasn't afraid. The main reason he feared these people was because they were related to Tyrian, not because they were vampires. None of them would hurt him, and even if they tried, Tyrian would step in. Madison trusted Tyrian to keep him safe, and he didn't think he'd ever regret trusting him.

"Just watch the movie."

Madison had tried, but he couldn't ignore the fact that he was the center of attention. The people around him were faking watching the movie, but they kept peeking at him and Tyrian as if they were an exotic display at the zoo or something.

Madison kept glancing at Tyrian. He'd gone from not knowing what to think of the vampire to having a crush on him to apparently being his boyfriend. It had been a whirlwind, and he still wasn't used to thinking of Tyrian as his.

Tyrian had no trouble with that. As soon as he and

Madison had sat on the couch, he'd wrapped an arm around Madison's shoulders and held him close, letting the others settle around them. It felt like he would never let Madison go, which was what Madison wanted.

"What do you think of the naiads?" one of the women in the room asked.

Madison was pretty sure her name was Yvonne. He felt he needed the family to wear name tags, at least initially. There were too many of them, and the only one he was sure about was Meyer. As to everyone else, Madison had no idea whether or not he was right when it came to their names.

"They're sneaky," Meyer said. "Did I tell you about the time two of them tried to kill me?"

One of the men laughed. "They did what we all wish we could do."

Meyer threw a popcorn kernel at the man's face. Madison squinted, trying to remember the guy's name, impressed when he caught the popcorn with his mouth. Vampires didn't need to eat, but apparently it wasn't a problem if they did, and they'd decided they couldn't watch the movie without popcorn.

But they weren't watching the movie. They were alternating between staring at Madison and talking about random stuff, but he didn't mind. He was here to get to know Tyrian's family, not to watch a movie, and the insight into their minds was fascinating.

They were vampires, but they were no different from shifters. They were fiercely protective of the people they loved, and apparently that now included Madison. They were visibly happy that Tyrian had found someone to love, and Madison was pretty sure they would defend him from anyone because of that. He wasn't even sure most of them liked him. They didn't know him yet, so they didn't have a reason to. They just wanted Tyrian to be happy, and they could see that

Madison did that.

He had no idea how. He *wanted* to make Tyrian happy, but he didn't know if he had it in him to do that. He should focus on getting his sister back, not on how being in Tyrian's arms felt, but it had been so long since he'd had something just for himself. Was it selfish?

"That's Rex," Tyrian whispered. "And the woman who asked about the naiads is Yvonne."

Madison was relieved that Tyrian was helping him and pleased he'd gotten Yvonne's name correctly. "There are so many of them," he whispered back.

Tyrian chuckled. "Not really."

"You turned nine people into vampires, and they all consider you their father. You have nine kids, Tyrian. That *is* a lot."

Tyrian chuckled and kissed the top of Madison's head. "Maybe you're right. I suppose I do consider all of them my children, even though technically, they're not mine."

"I think they're yours in all the ways that count."

Tyrian was silent for a moment. "I suppose you're right. It's a nice way to see it."

"It's the only way there is. From what I've seen of your relationship with them, you're more a father to them than my biological father ever was to me or Katie. That's what counts, not the fact that you didn't bring them into this world. Besides, you kind of did. You brought them into your vampire world, and I think that's what matters the most to them."

Madison had been watching just him and his mother for most of his life. After Katie had been born ten years ago, it had been Madison and her. He'd expected that to never change, especially after their father had dragged them away from the pack, but he'd been wrong. It would take time for him to consider the people surrounding him in the living room a family, but if he and Tyrian were going to be together, that was what they would be to each other.

Family.

A door slammed, making Madison jump. No one seemed worried for a few seconds, but then a man burst into the living room. The siblings were on their feet in seconds, all of them moving toward the man. Madison had seen him around pack territory, so he knew he was another of the siblings. His blond curls were messy, and his blue eyes were wide. He looked like one of those angels in the paintings, or at least he would have if it hadn't been clear he was terrified.

"They're attacking," he declared.

Tyrian quickly got to his feet. "Alpin?"

Right, that was Alpin, the boyfriend of the dragon shifter who wanted to eat Madison. Merrick glared at him every time he saw him, and Madison made sure to spend as much time away from him as he could. He wasn't about to tempt fate, especially with a dragon.

"It's all over the news. They're attacking the mall and not being sneaky about it. Everyone can see the dragons. They're killing humans, Tyrian."

Tyrian looked around the room. "We're going." He turned to Madison, who quickly got to his feet. "Stay here. We'll be back as soon as we can."

Madison was having none of that. "I'm coming with you."

"You can't."

"I can, and now isn't the moment to fight about it. Everyone's going, and I'm not staying back. I might not be a dragon shifter or a vampire, but it doesn't mean I can't help." And Madison *wanted* to help. If the pack was going to be his family again, if he was going to belong, he needed to show them that he cared. He had to be there when the pack needed him.

And right now, they did.

Tyrian swallowed his fear and the words that had been about

to cross his lips. He wanted to order Madison not to move from the house, maybe even to leave Meyer behind to keep an eye on him. He was terrified something would happen to him, and the thought made him panic.

But he couldn't keep Madison here against his will. It wouldn't be fair, and it might destroy their relationship. Besides, Tyrian never wanted to be that controlling with anyone, least of all the man he was falling in love with.

That meant Madison was coming with him and the others.

"You need to be careful," he told Madison. "Fay still believes you're working for her, which means she might think it weird to see you there."

Madison shook his head. "She's not going to think it's weird when it's clear the pack needs everyone on board to help. It'll make sense that Kieran pulled me in, especially if people are dying."

"I don't want anything to happen to you," Tyrian murmured.

"And I don't want anything to happen to you or your family. There's no way to know what will happen, but we can fight together and be there for each other. I'll watch your back, and you can watch mine, all right?"

Tyrian nodded because he didn't have a choice. Madison was coming with them, whether Tyrian wanted him to or not.

He turned to Alpin. "Tell me everything you know."

They were already moving toward the front door, ready to climb into their cars. Merrick was nowhere to be seen, which was odd, because Alpin was here.

"Merrick and Arlen shifted and headed there flying," Alpin said as he climbed into the back seat of the car Tyrian used. Meyer settled next to him while Madison got into the passenger seat. "Everyone else is going there, too."

"What's the clan doing?"

Meyer had his phone out. "They're attacking the mall and

killing the humans who try to get to safety." He sounded grim, which was how Tyrian felt.

The clan had finally made their move. They'd probably been planning this for weeks, if not longer. They'd exposed the supernatural world to humans in the worst way possible, and Tyrian wasn't sure anyone would survive it.

But right now, that didn't matter. They needed to get to the mall and help as much as they could. He had no doubt that many humans were already dead, but they could save others. It was the only way for them to be able to live with themselves, but also to show the humans that not all supernatural creatures and dragon shifters were bad people.

Tyrian had no idea what the world would look like once this mess was over, but they needed to do everything they could to ensure supernatural creatures wouldn't be hunted.

That was a worry for another day. Right now, their focus had to be on the mall, and Tyrian dreaded what they'd find there.

He knew he'd been right to feel that way when they finally reached it.

Tyrian had never been inside it, but he'd driven past it several times. It wasn't massive, but in such a small town, it was where people gathered. There were stores and a theater, and the fact that this was a weekend evening meant the place had been packed.

Which in turn meant there were many bodies already stretched out on the ground.

Tyrian swallowed. He'd seen violence many times over the hundreds of years he'd been alive. He'd seen shifters cut off vampires' heads, vampires tearing out people's throats, and many other things that still plagued his nightmares. This was worse than all of that.

Tyrian parked the car in the first spot he could find in front of the mall and stared. Half of the building had crumbled and was on fire. He didn't know what the dragons had done, but it seemed almost as if they'd landed something massively heavy on top of the building. There was smoke and fire everywhere, cars twisted and burning, and of course, dead bodies.

There was a woman not far from the car. She was on her back, her arms spread, her open eyes staring at the sky. She didn't move, didn't even blink, and she never would again.

She was dead.

"This is horrible," Madison muttered.

"You should stay in the car." Tyrian turned toward him, relieved to have a distraction.

But of course, Madison would have none of that. "I'm not staying in the car. It's not going to help me avoid seeing horrible things, and I can help."

Tyrian wanted to shield him from the horrors of the world, but he couldn't, so instead, he nodded. "Everyone, keep your eyes open," he told his family as they gathered around him. "I don't know what Kieran expects us to do, but the dragons are still attacking. Stay out of their way and try to get as many people as possible to safety. Don't attack the dragons and stay away from the fire. I want to see all of you in one piece when we get back to the house later today."

Everyone nodded, but Tyrian couldn't help but wonder if he was about to lose one of his family members. The thought made him sick, but he wouldn't tell them to stay back. They'd tell him to fuck off, but even if they didn't, it wouldn't be like them not to help. They'd want to do everything they could, and it was why they were here, after all.

They scattered. Tyrian was relieved when Madison stuck close to him, but at the same time, he wished Madison didn't have to see any of this. He already had enough to deal with. It wasn't fair for him to be involved in this situation, but he'd made his decision, and Tyrian needed to respect that.

Hopefully, Madison was right, and Fay would believe Kieran had needed all hands on deck. At the moment, though, it didn't matter.

Several dragons were attacking the building, spitting fire and gripping bits and pieces with their claws to rip them away. A loud cry made Tyrian look up in time to see Merrick in his dragon form. He didn't slow down as he approached. Instead, he threw himself straight at the closest dragon, sending them tumbling toward the burning building.

Madison sucked in a breath. "Who's that?" he asked.

"Merrick."

Arlen was right behind him. Tyrian had learned to recognize them in their dragon form, thankfully. It meant he could tell how they were doing and that they weren't the dragons getting hurt.

"They'll take care of the dragons. We need to see if there are survivors still in the building and get them out."

Madison set his jaw and nodded. "Let's go."

They made their way toward the part of the building that was still intact, but it wasn't easy. People were screaming and running, at least when they could. Most of them were covered in dirt and had burns on their bodies.

But not all of them were running. People were on the ground, unconscious or in pain. Madison and Tyrian grabbed the nearest people and took them to a safer place in the parking lot. Then they went back in, grabbed the next survivors, and repeated the process. Magda and Parker stayed with the survivors, trying to help them as well as they could. Nobody could do anything while the dragons were still attacking, and Tyrian was starting to wonder if Arlen and Merrick would be enough. They were only two dragons, while the clan was massive, or at least, it felt like it, looking at the carnage.

A loud screech made Tyrian look up. Another dragon had appeared, but their behavior was odd. They could only be a clan dragon. Instead of helping their clan members against Arlen and Merrick, they were trying to place themselves between them as if to protect Arlen and Merrick.

"There's Meyer," Madison said as he rushed forward. He grabbed a woman from Meyer's arms and rushed her into the parking garage. Meyer and Tyrian nodded at each other, and Meyer turned back toward the mall, stepping inside. Tyrian moved to follow, but the sound of something heavy slamming against the building made him look up.

The new dragon who'd tried putting himself between Arlen, Merrick, and the clan, was down. One of the dragons Tyrian didn't recognize had them pinned, but their weight was too much for the burning building. It started collapsing, dust flying everywhere as it creaked and cracked.

Tyrian called out for Meyer, and he saw Meyer turn around, but the entrance collapsed before he could run to him. For a split second, he simply stood in place, speechless.

Madison turned just in time to see that Meyer was inside when the building collapsed, and he ran forward, pushing past his boyfriend. There was too much dust, and he couldn't see much. "Meyer?" he called out, desperate to find the man.

He liked Meyer. He didn't want Tyrian to lose any of his family members, but it wasn't just that. Meyer had been nice to him, even when he'd thought Madison was a traitor. He couldn't be dead.

A hand grabbed Madison's shoulder and pulled him back. Tyrian had finally snapped out of it, but instead of going in and trying to find Meyer, he was pulling Madison away.

Madison shook off his shoulder. "I have to get in there."

"You're going to get yourself killed."

"I don't care. Meyer was inside, and I'm not leaving him there."

Tyrian glowered at him.

Madison expected him to refuse his help, so he was surprised when he finally nodded. "We'll get him together."

That was more than Madison had expected, and he knew he couldn't do this on his own, anyway. "We need to get to him." He stared at the mall, searching for a way. The front part had collapsed, but he could still see openings big enough to sneak through.

But not in his human form.

He took off his shirt. It was dirty with blood and things he didn't want to think about, but he'd need it once this was over, even though he'd rather burn it than put it on again. "I'm going to shift."

Tyrian stared at him with wide eyes.

It felt good being in charge, for once. It made him feel more in control, even though nothing in his life was.

"Are you sure?" Tyrian asked. He took Madison's shirt when Madison handed it to him.

Tyrian had never seen Madison naked—he tried not to think about that. Even when he'd helped him wash up, Madison had never been fully naked. He'd thought and hoped the circumstances would be different, but it didn't matter.

"I'll be able to find him more easily if I'm a wolf. Besides, I was always sticking my nose into tight spaces when I was a kid. I'll be fine."

He stood naked and prepared himself to shift, but Tyrian stopped him before he could.

"Be careful," he said.

"Always. I'll find him, and I'll bring him back." Madison prayed it was a promise he could keep.

He shifted as quickly as possible. He wanted to sniff at Tyrian and maybe rub against him a little so he'd smell like him, but there was no time. Instead, Madison ran toward the building. He could still hear the dragons fighting in the sky but was too afraid to look.

Merrick didn't like him, and Madison didn't think he liked Merrick much, but that didn't matter. Merrick was Alpin's boyfriend, and Alpin was one of Tyrian's children. Madison didn't want anything to happen to Merrick, not just because he was family. Merrick was on their side, and while he was grumpy, it didn't mean he was a bad person. He wanted to protect the pack, and so did Madison.

He wiggled through one of the openings. It was a tight fit, but like he'd told Tyrian, he was used to fitting into tight spaces. Digging through the debris took work, and he had to stop several times to catch his breath, but soon he caught Meyer's scent. He let it guide him around collapsed walls and columns, and he was relieved to see that while the front part of the mall had collapsed, the part behind it was still mostly standing. The problem was that Meyer wasn't there. No, he was under the rubble.

Madison started digging again. It was the only way to get to Meyer, and while it hurt his paws, he eventually managed to clear a large enough space. He wiggled his way through that, too, heading down and following the scent.

"I hope to god that you're a shifter and not a wild wolf," a voice eventually said.

Madison whimpered in relief. He wanted to tell Meyer it was him, but in this form, he couldn't.

It looked like when the building had collapsed, Meyer had thrown himself into a hallway that led to the bathroom. The mall had collapsed around him, but he appeared to be all right, even though he was stuck.

Finally, Madison managed to get through. There was enough space here for him to shift, as long as he stayed on his knees, so he quickly did, wincing when his human skin pressed against bits of plaster and glass.

"Shit, Madison," Meyer said. "You should shift back.

You're going to hurt yourself."

Meyer was right, so Madison obeyed. He inched closer, then licked Meyer's cheek.

Meyer looked startled, but he grinned. "I'm going to tell Tyrian you kissed me."

Madison grinned, then licked his cheek again. He couldn't save Meyer by himself. Meyer's human body was too big to be able to sneak around the way Madison had, which meant he was stuck. The only thing Madison could do was keep him company, so he settled against Meyer's side.

He didn't know how much time passed, but they eventually heard loud noises from above them. Madison squeezed his body closer to Meyer's, and together, they looked up.

Plaster rained over their faces. Madison sneezed, then rubbed a paw over his nose. A hole appeared in the ceiling, and a massive dragon head peeked through.

Madison swallowed. He wasn't sure if this dragon belonged to the pack or the clan, but he felt Meyer relax, so he could take a wild guess.

"That's Merrick," Meyer said.

Madison was pretty sure Merrick would happily eat him if he realized who he was, so he wasn't entirely reassured, but it was better than a clan dragon finding them.

Merrick continued working, pulling away massive chunks of walls. They had to be careful because there were powerlines in the rubble, but Madison was pretty sure the power had been cut. He couldn't see any lights on, which made his position deep in the rubble even worse.

Someone else appeared. Tyrian climbed down toward them, slipping and almost falling several times. Madison watched him carefully, relieved when he finally reached them as Merrick widened the hole.

Madison got to his feet, shook his fur, then went to lick Tyrian's hand.

Tyrian rubbed the top of Madison's head but wasted no time. "Let's get Meyer out."

The three of them had to work together. The hole Merrick had made was in the ceiling—what was left of it, anyway. That meant they had to climb, and while it was fairly easy for Madison in his wolf form, the same couldn't be said for Tyrian and Meyer. He went back several times to help them, but eventually, they reached the hole in the ceiling.

Madison scrambled out, then immediately turned around and shifted. When Tyrian's hand appeared, Madison grabbed it and pulled him out. Then Tyrian turned to Meyer.

That was when Madison realized Meyer had been hurt. He wasn't sure how he'd missed that, considering how much blood was seeping from Meyer's side, but he supposed it had been easy to ignore because of the dust and the blood so many people had lost. Now, it wasn't.

Meyer clutched his side as he moved. He stumbled, but Tyrian was there to keep him upright. Tyrian looked around frantically, and Madison knew what was needed.

He stepped forward, ready to offer Meyer his wrist, but someone beat him to it.

"He needs blood, right?" Ollis asked as he pushed past Madison.

Tyrian nodded. "Urgently. Having blood will help him heal."

Ollis thrust his wrist out. "He can have mine."

Tyrian stared at him for a moment. "Are you sure?"

"I wouldn't be offering otherwise. Come on. Get him to bite me."

Madison had liked Ollis before, but now, he could kiss him. Instead, he waited until Ollis and Meyer were settled together, then moved forward and kissed Tyrian.

Tyrian felt better as soon as he had Madison in his arms. It didn't matter that Madison was naked and that they were both covered in dust, blood, and other nasty things. They were safe, and Meyer would be all right.

Tyrian wrapped his arms around Madison's body but kept the kiss short. The fight wasn't over, and they needed to be careful.

"We need to leave," Merrick ordered.

Tyrian hadn't noticed him shifting back, which was a feat considering how big Merrick was in his dragon form.

"There are more people in there," Tyrian protested.

"I know, but humans are coming."

"They're already here wounded and dying," Madison pointed out.

Merrick glared at him. "*More* of them are coming. Firefighters and police, all of that. Kieran ordered the pack to head back home because he doesn't want any of us to be caught in this."

Tyrian looked around. There were many dead, but there were also many survivors, and it was thanks to them. He didn't want recognition. He just cared that he'd helped people and saved a few lives.

They had their orders. Kieran had asked them to retreat to pack territory, so they would.

Tyrian had no idea what would happen now that humans knew about shifters. He wasn't even sure what they knew. At the very least, they were now aware that dragons existed, but had they seen any of them shift into their human form? Maybe they'd believe that dragons were animals and had attacked without reason. Tyrian wasn't sure that would be the best outcome to this mess, but there was nothing he could do to change any of this. Whatever humans wanted to believe, they would believe.

He ushered Madison toward the edge of the roof. Merrick

had to shift back to get them down safely, and while he didn't look happy about helping Madison, he did so without anyone having to ask. Tyrian was relieved, just like he was relieved to see that the rest of his family had made it out in one piece and were gathered in the parking garage.

"Let's go," he said, guiding Madison toward the car. He'd dropped Madison's clothes somewhere, and he wasn't about to stay back to look for them. They couldn't afford to waste time.

They clambered into the car, squeezing in together. Merrick was still with them, as was Ollis. For some reason, the wolf shifter seemed especially worried about Meyer, and while Tyrian wanted to reassure him that Meyer would be all right, he couldn't.

He didn't know if Meyer would be.

Meyer had taken blood, and now, they could only wait for him to heal. He was pale but awake and softly talking to Ollis, which Tyrian decided was a good thing.

On the other hand, Merrick's expression was thunderous. He glared at everything and everyone around him, and it was good that he was in the back seat, because Madison looked terrified of him.

They were silent until they reached pack territory. Tyrian drove straight to the house he shared with his family, because Meyer would need to rest, and Merrick could walk or even fly to Kieran's home or wherever the others had gone.

None of them had noticed the dragon following them.

The dragon landed as soon as Tyrian parked in front of the house. It shook the ground under the car, and Tyrian jerked his arm out to keep Madison safe in his seat. Merrick was out of the car before anyone could say anything, and Tyrian scrambled to follow.

He thought the dragons would start fighting, but the dragon who'd followed them shifted back into his human form. He was a man with long brown hair and wild eyes. He was wounded, blood seeping from his shoulder, but he didn't seem to care as he raised his hands.

"I'm not here to fight," he said.

Merrick didn't care. He threw himself at the dragon, and Tyrian had to run to get in between them. He didn't get there before Merrick punched the dragon in the face, and the dragon stumbled back.

He didn't punch Merrick back. He didn't even try to defend himself. Instead, he raised his hands as if to show he wasn't a danger.

Tyrian wasn't sure about that, but he still put himself between the dragon and Merrick, pushing back against Merrick's chest when he tried to get past him.

"Leave him alone," he snapped.

"He's part of the clan," Merrick said with a growl.

Luckily, Tyrian wasn't the only one who tried to stop Merrick. Arlen landed next to them, and a few seconds later, he stood in front of Merrick in his human form. Together, he and Tyrian managed to keep Merrick away from the dragon, but Tyrian was worried. This dragon didn't belong with the pack, which meant Merrick was right—he was with the clan. He could be a danger to Madison, and Tyrian had to keep Madison safe.

"He helped us," Arlen said, trying to get through to Merrick.

"He's with the clan," Merrick repeated.

"Because I don't have anywhere else to go," the dragon said. "Please. Just give me a chance, all right? Listen to what I have to say. I promise I'm not here to hurt the pack or you."

"*Why* are you here?" Tyrian asked, turning to him.

The dragon looked him up and down. Tyrian grinned, exposing his fangs so the dragon would know what he was. He didn't think the dragon was afraid of him, but having all the cards on the table was good.

"I'm Luca," the dragon said.

At the moment, Tyrian didn't care about the dragon's name. Still, it was ingrained in him to be polite. "I'm Tyrian."

"I didn't want to be involved in the attack. In fact, I tried to stop it and save people," Luca said in a rush. "And now the clan knows I'm working against them, and they're going to kill me if I go back."

"Do you think we care?" Merrick asked.

Tyrian had to resist the urge to roll his eyes. He kept his focus on Luca, trying to figure out whether the dragon was attempting to fool them into trusting him or if he truly wanted out.

Tyrian knew what he'd want if he were in Luca's situation. He wouldn't want to stay with the clan, especially after the attack on the mall. But like Madison, Luca could be a spy, and there was no way for them to know for sure.

"I'm not the alpha of this pack," Tyrian explained. "I can listen to what you have to say, but I won't be the one making decisions."

Luca nodded. "At least you're willing to listen. I just want out of the clan, please. What they're doing is too much, and I disagree with all of it. I don't want to deal lethal drugs. I don't want to kill other supernatural creatures or humans. I don't care about power or territory or even money. I just want to be free."

It made sense. Luca was saying the right words, but it was hard to believe him. Still, just like they'd given Madison a chance, Tyrian felt they should give Luca one. He wouldn't be the one to decide that, but if Kieran asked for his opinion, he'd tell him he believed Luca meant well.

He'd seen Luca fight his clan members. He could have easily gotten killed, and in fact, he was visibly hurt. Tyrian doubted the clan would act like Fay had with Madison. They wouldn't be sneaky about wanting to destroy the pack. They didn't need a spy. They had more than enough manpower to destroy the pack entirely, and it was anyone's guess why they hadn't yet.

But maybe Luca could give them insight into that. Even if he couldn't, abandoning him wouldn't be fair, especially when he'd tried to help.

Tyrian sighed. "Follow us into our house. We'll lock you in a bedroom and keep an eye on you until the alpha can see you. If you try anything, you're done."

"I'm not going to attack or try to escape," Luca promised.

"Fine." Because even if he did try to attack or escape, there was nothing the vampires could do against him. A dragon shifter in their dragon form was much too powerful and massive, and he could kill them all.

But he hadn't yet, and Tyrian had to believe he wouldn't. Maybe he had too much faith in people and only saw the good in them, but he wasn't willing to change that.

Especially not when that inclination had given him Madison.

Chapter Six

M adison had been checking the news obsessively. He didn't know what he expected to see, especially after what happened at the mall. There had been footage of the dragons attacking, but so far, it seemed like no one knew they were shifters. Humans were understandably freaking out even though they thought the dragons were animals.

They weren't the only ones. Madison was freaking out, too. He still didn't have Katie. He hadn't heard from Fay since the attack, even though he'd tried calling her several times. He didn't know how else to get to her, and he was starting to wonder if something had happened to Katie.

He'd never forgive himself in that case. He should have done more to get her back and to make sure she wouldn't get hurt, but even now, he didn't know what else he could have done. He'd done everything Fay had asked except for betraying the pack, but she didn't know that.

Madison had suspected that Fay never intended to let him and Katie go, but he hadn't wanted to believe it. Now, he couldn't avoid thinking about it, no matter how much he wanted to. It was the reality he had to deal with, but it didn't mean he was letting go of the dream of getting his sister back.

He *would* get her back. He just didn't know how he'd do it.

"Nothing has changed," a gentle voice said.

Madison tilted his head against the couch to see Tyrian standing behind it. He was carrying a plate and a glass, and they weren't for him. He rarely ate or drank anything, even when he was with Madison.

Madison sighed. "I know, but what if something happens and I'm not watching?" he asked as he sat up straighter.

Tyrian walked around the couch to sit next to him. He handed him the glass, then the plate, and Madison couldn't help but smile.

Tyrian had brought him a muffin and a glass of milk.

Since they'd gotten together, he'd been feeding Madison like there was no tomorrow. Madison would be the first to admit he'd needed feeding, especially after he'd been forced to leave the pack. His meals hadn't been regular when his family lived here, and that hadn't improved after they left. More importantly, the fact that Tyrian was feeding him was a sign of how much he cared. It was how Tyrian showed his love. He cared for people, protected them, and ensured they had what they needed. Madison had known Tyrian cared, but it felt good to see it in action.

He balanced the plate on his lap and drank some of the milk. He knew what Tyrian was saying. Obsessing over what was happening wouldn't help him get Katie back. It certainly wouldn't help him sleep better at night.

The problem was that he didn't know what else to do, and it was both terrifying and frustrating. Every time he closed his eyes, he wondered what Fay was doing to Katie. He didn't know how to deal with that or with the knowledge that he might never see her again.

"Have you heard from Fay?" Tyrian asked.

Madison shook his head. "I've tried calling her, but her phone is always off." He hesitated, unsure if he wanted to ask the question that was bothering him. "Do you think she hurt Katie? That she's on the run and left everyone else behind?"

"I don't."

Tyrian's answer was instant, and it made Madison feel better, even though Tyrian didn't know anything more than he did.

"Why not?" It was better to listen to Tyrian than to the TV because there was nothing good on the news.

"She wants the pack. That's why she left, and she's not going to give it up easily. Besides, no matter what happened at the mall, it doesn't change anything for her. The mall was the clan. Her objective is the pack."

"But she's stopped attacking pack businesses."

"She's lying low, which makes sense. Everyone's freaking out over dragons being real. She probably doesn't want any human to stumble onto wolf shifters by accident. It would be too easy for someone in town to see them, and then what would happen?"

Madison shrugged. He didn't care what would happen, even though he should. He only cared about his sister.

Once he was done eating, he put the plate and glass on the coffee table and snatched his phone. Without hoping for much, he called Fay again. She'd have to answer eventually, right? If she wanted to find out what he knew, she'd have to.

This time, the call got through instead of going straight to voicemail.

Madison shot up from his slouch. His heart hammered, and he could have sworn he could hear it. He listened to the phone ringing, holding his breath while Tyrian tried to get his attention, no doubt to make sure he was all right.

He didn't think he was.

"What the fuck do you want?" Fay wasted no time.

Madison could have cried in relief. "Where's Katie? How is she? Why haven't you been answering your phone?"

"We've been a little busy. I'm sure you have television, so you should know."

Fay sounded snarky, but also exhausted. That made Madison wonder what the dragons were having her do, but to be honest, he didn't care. He just wanted to know how Katie was.

He was so done with all of this. Was it too much to ask for

him to be allowed to live his life in peace? He supposed that even if Fay let him go, there were no certainties that he could have that. The dragons might still attack, and so could Fay.

But he and Katie would be together. He'd be able to protect her, and that was all that mattered. She was the reason he was doing this. She was the person Madison cared the most about in the entire world, and he'd had enough of her being in danger.

"I need to see you," he told Fay.

"No. You need to stay with the pack and continue spying on them, no matter what those damn dragons did."

"I don't care about the dragons, and this is important. I have information and can't tell you on the phone."

"Why not? You're talking to me on the phone right now."

"Because I don't trust you not to have hurt my sister."

"Or is it because the vampire you've been spending so much time with is with you?"

Madison swallowed. He'd known she had spies, so he wasn't surprised they'd seen him with Tyrian. "It's not my fault Kieran doesn't trust me and assigned me a guard," he said bitterly, even though nothing could be further from the truth.

"How are you getting your information if you have a guard?"

"It's one of the reasons I need to see you. I'll be at the old motel in an hour. Bring Katie with you."

Madison didn't want to give Fay the opportunity to argue, so he hung up. He stared at the phone for a moment, asking himself what he'd done.

What if she hurt Katie? She didn't care about Katie or Madison. She cared about getting what she wanted and wouldn't hesitate to hurt people if it meant getting it.

Madison had always known that eventually, Fay would get rid of him and Katie. Right now, they were useful, but once they weren't anymore, she wouldn't hesitate. That meant that Madison needed to get to Katie before that happened, and he hoped he would be able to.

"I'm proud of you," Tyrian murmured.

Madison chuckled. The sound was slightly hysterical, so he clamped his lips together. "I'm an idiot. What if instead of bringing Katie, she hurts her?"

"You're still useful to her, but you wouldn't be if your sister was gone," Tyrian pointed out. "I don't know what's happening with Fay and her people, but she needs you."

And she was the one person Madison wouldn't care about disappointing. In fact, he *wanted* her to be disappointed, because if she wasn't, it would mean that she got what she wanted, and that wasn't something he could deal with.

"I need to go," he told Tyrian.

"You're not going alone."

Madison grinned. "I never expected to. I know you, Tyrian. You wouldn't let me go on my own even if I begged you."

Tyrian seemed satisfied that Madison realized that. "Good. We need to come up with a plan."

Madison wanted to say no and hide his head in the sand, but he couldn't. Tyrian was doing this to help him, and they could get Katie back.

But they'd have to work together, something Madison wasn't used to. His first instinct was still to hide what he was about to do, even though he trusted Tyrian.

He needed to take a chance on Tyrian—on them—and he needed to do it now.

Tyrian wasn't surprised that Madison had given Fay an ultimatum. He'd been trying to reach her for days, and he'd been frantic about not being able to. The situation meant that he'd imagined what might have happened to his sister too many times, and now, he'd had enough. He wanted Katie back, and he would get her.

Tyrian would make sure of it.

"When you told her you'd meet her at the old motel, do you mean the one where you were staying before?" he asked as he got to his feet. They needed to plan. Maybe they could have an entire team there, hiding and keeping an eye on what was happening.

"Yeah. I don't know where else to look for her and Katie. We're not taking in a team, though."

Tyrian wasn't surprised that Madison could tell what he was thinking. "It's the only thing we can do. Fay might hurt you or Katie otherwise."

"She could hurt us whether I go alone or with a team. She doesn't trust me, Tyrian. Besides, she has people who saw me with you. She's going to expect you to be there, at the very least."

"You'll tell her you managed to lose me."

"And you think she'd going to believe that?"

"Since it's afternoon and you told her you'd meet her in an hour, yes."

Madison shook his head instantly. "The sun will hurt you."

"It'll bother me, but it won't hurt me. I'll cover myself as much as possible and slather my skin in sunscreen." It wouldn't last forever, but it would give him enough time to do what he needed to do.

"I can't put anyone else in danger, especially not you," Madison whispered.

Tyrian strode toward him. "You're not putting me in danger. I know what I'm getting into, and I'm offering to help you and your sister. I know I don't look like much when it comes to fighting, but I've been alive for a long time, Madison. I know what I'm doing." Even if Tyrian and Madison went alone, Tyrian was convinced he could do this. He doubted Fay would have many people with her. She sounded secretive, which made sense considering she'd betrayed her pack, and she probably feared someone would betray her now.

That was what scared people the most—for someone to do to them what they did to others. It was a kind of projection they didn't know how to deal with, and Madison didn't seem to understand that. He knew they didn't trust him, but he didn't suspect the depth of what Fay was ready to do to get rid of him. He wasn't going anywhere on his own, no matter what Tyrian had to do or say to convince him of that.

"And we're not going alone," he said. "I'll take the two oldest of my children. They'll stay back unless we need them, but they'll be there."

Madison was already shaking his head. "I can't put someone else in danger."

"What you can't do is go there on your own. Fay has to expect you'll betray her, which means she'll believe you're not there alone. I think she expects Kieran to be there, maybe other wolf shifters. Having vampires with you will be a surprise, and we need that element. She won't expect us there because it's the middle of the day, but we'll be there, and we'll get Katie."

Madison's eyes were wide. "I just don't want anyone to be hurt because of me."

Tyrian moved closer to him and took his hand. "Even if someone does get hurt, and I don't think they will, it won't be your fault. It will be Fay's fault. I need you to understand that. You never wanted any of this to happen or anyone to be hurt. Your heart is big and caring."

"You make me sound like someone else."

Tyrian smiled. "Because you don't see yourself the way I see you. You're brave and caring. You're stubborn and incredibly sweet, always ready to give someone a chance to show you that they don't mean harm. It wasn't easy for you to deal with any of this, and you're in this situation because of your father. You didn't have a choice. I do, as do my children. I'm choosing to come with you to protect you and your sister. I won't force anyone to come along, but I have no doubt they'll volunteer."

"Why would they do that?"

Madison truly didn't seem to understand. Considering the family he'd grown up with, that made sense. From what he'd told Tyrian, his father had never been much of a father. Hell, Madison had been more of a father to Katie than their biological father ever had. He didn't understand loyalty or helping people without a reason.

Besides, Tyrian's children had a very good reason to help Madison.

Tyrian took out his phone and quickly texted Yvonne and Parker. He wished he could ask Meyer to come because he was close to Madison, but he was much younger than Yvonne and Parker, and Tyrian didn't want anyone to risk getting hurt. The others would probably bitch about not being allowed to come along, but they'd understand and respect Tyrian's decision.

"They would do it because they care about me," Tyrian eventually explained. "And you matter to me like no one else has ever mattered. That's what's important to them. You make me happy, and they don't want me to lose that."

"I don't understand how I can make you happy," Madison whispered.

Tyrian pulled him into his arms. He kissed the top of his head and closed his eyes, praying that everything would be okay. "How could you not make me happy? You're a sweet man who's been dealt a horrible hand by life. Yet, you've done everything you could to make it out. Even more importantly, you've done everything you could to make your sister happy and keep her safe. I don't know if she realizes how lucky she is considering she's so young, but eventually, she will. She'll be able to see that you protected her from your father. She'll understand how many sacrifices you made."

"You make me sound like someone I'm not," Madison whispered.

"But you *are* all those things, even though you don't see yourself that way. You're not only brave and caring. You're also stubborn and sweet, you give people a chance even when you're scared, and you never gave up. I love how resilient you are and at the same time, I wish you didn't have to be. I love *you*, Madison, and while I understand you don't know what to do with that and that you don't see it, it's not going to change. It's how I feel, and I'll do whatever I can to make you happy, as will my family."

"I'm too young to be a stepfather to adults," Madison muttered. His voice was muffled against Tyrian's chest.

Tyrian laughed. "I'm pretty sure at least a few of them would try to bite your fingers off if you attempted to be a step-father to them. I talk about them as my children, but they were already adults when I turned them into vampires."

Madison peered up. "That doesn't mean they're not your kids."

"I suppose they are." And to Tyrian, who'd always wanted a big family, it was heaven. He loved having children, but now that he was with Madison, he could imagine them having kids who were actually children.

But not before Katie was back with them and not before Fay had been dealt with. No matter how much Tyrian wanted this, he had things to deal with first and was ready for it to finally end.

"You called?" Parker asked as he strode into the living room.

Madison tried to pull away from Tyrian, but Tyrian didn't let him. He didn't care who saw them together. Besides,

Parker and Yvonne were his children, and like he'd told Madison, they wanted him to be happy.

"Madison is going to meet Fay. He asked that his sister be there, and I need help to keep him safe and to get her back."

Parker didn't ask why they were doing this. He didn't argue that he wasn't up for it. Instead, he nodded, his expression grim. "What do you expect from me?"

"And from me?" Yvonne asked, walking in.

Tyrian looked at both of them, then down at Madison. "I expect you to make sure Madison and Katie make it back home in one piece."

They needed to start planning, so he guided Madison toward the couch.

They didn't have much time, but they didn't *need* much time. They'd do this, and once Katie was back, Madison would finally settle down with the pack.

And so would Tyrian.

Madison couldn't say he was surprised that Yvonne and Parker were so eager to help. He wouldn't have asked anything of them, but he wasn't the one who had. Tyrian was, and none of Tyrian's children said no when he asked something of them.

Madison couldn't begin to imagine what Tyrian meant to them. He didn't feel any kind of loyalty when it came to his father or Fay, and he never would, but it was clear that Tyrian's children would do anything for him.

Which was why the two of them were headed toward the motel where Madison had lived after leaving the pack.

He was glad he wouldn't have to stick around this time. The motel was a mess and had been abandoned for a good reason. A pipe had burst somewhere and had been too expensive to fix. Fay had been giddy when she'd realized they could

106

stay there without anyone kicking them out, but the place had been dirty and abandoned, and even worse, it had been full of mold. Madison had been terrified for Katie, and he didn't like that she had to go back there, but it wouldn't be for long.

Because she was coming home with him. He wouldn't have it any other way.

He was driving, for once. He and Tyrian had agreed that he'd stop the car before they reached the motel to let Tyrian out. He'd meet up with Yvonne and Parker, who were coming in with their own car, just in case. Madison would continue toward the motel on his own, or rather, it would look like he was on his own.

But he wouldn't be.

Madison was still nervous. It would be too easy for something bad to happen, and he had to force himself not to obsess over how wrong things could go. He'd have to fight Fay for Katie, but he was ready to do it. He just wanted out of this situation, and he wanted it to happen now. He was done fake spying on the pack for Fay, going along with what she wanted, and putting himself and his sister in danger.

"There," Tyrian said. "You can let me out here."

Madison slowed the car. He tightened his hands around the steering wheel but didn't beg Tyrian not to leave. He knew Tyrian wouldn't be going far and that he'd keep an eye on him the entire time, but it was still hard when he'd feel like he was alone.

Madison was used to being alone, but he hadn't been since he'd arrived back in pack territory. It had been a shock after so many years, but he loved it and couldn't imagine his life any differently now. He had everything he wanted, and in a way, it was thanks to Fay.

She'd be so pissed if she ever found out about that.

"Don't try looking around for me or the others," Tyrian ordered. "Fay will notice if you do, and she'll get suspicious.

You don't need to look for us, anyway. We'll be there whether you see us or not."

"I know. You'd never abandon me to do this on my own."

"Damn right, and they wouldn't, either." Tyrian hesitated, then leaned over to kiss Madison. "You're everything I've ever wanted in my long life, and I'm not giving you up. I'm not allowing you to get hurt. No matter how scared or worried you are, I'm watching over you, and I want you to remember that."

Madison felt a bit flustered. "Like my guardian angel?"

Tyrian grinned. "More like a guardian vampire."

Madison was still worried, but Tyrian's words made it easier to focus. He just had to do this. Once he did, he and Katie would be free. That was all he wanted.

Leaving Tyrian behind still felt like leaving part of his heart. Madison did his best not to focus on that feeling or on what might be about to happen. Luckily, the motel wasn't far, so he didn't have to worry for long.

He parked in front of the building and looked up at it. He didn't think he was imagining the fact that it had gotten worse since the last time he'd been there, and he hoped Fay hadn't stashed Katie in one of the rooms. Knowing her, she'd probably have picked the worst one just because she knew it would freak Madison out.

She wasn't a good person. She'd always looked up to her father, and he was an asshole. It was good that he wasn't the alpha anymore and that Fay would never be one. The pack was in good hands with Kieran, and they were finally healing from everything his father had done.

Now if Fay would just leave them alone, it would be perfect.

Madison sucked in a breath and got out of the car. He wasn't about to go into the rooms, so he stayed by the car, his heart racing and his palms damp. He looked around and listened, trying to find out where Fay might be hiding, but he didn't have to wonder for long.

The office door office slammed open. Madison had to force himself not to run to Katie when he saw her stumbling out of the office. Fay was behind her, squeezing her shoulder hard enough to make her knuckles go white.

But as worried as Madison was for Katie, that wasn't what made his stomach drop. No, that was his father, who came out of the office behind Fay.

Madison swallowed. He'd expected Fay to do something like this, so he wasn't surprised by his father's presence. The problem was that he didn't know how to deal with it. Seeing his father made him want to scream and run away, but he couldn't.

So instead of looking at him, he focused on Katie.

Her hair was tangled as if it hadn't been brushed in a while. Her cheeks were flushed, and there was a streak of dirt on her left cheek. She was crying, and she sobbed even harder when she saw Madison but wasn't allowed to go to him.

"Maddie," she screamed.

Madison forced himself to smile. "Hey, chickpea. I'm glad to see you're okay."

She seemed to be. She was dirty, and Madison was ready to bet she hadn't been fed much, but he'd take care of all of that as soon as he had her home.

Which meant he had to deal with Fay and his father.

He turned his attention to them. "You said you were going to take care of her," he accused.

Fay grinned. "I did. I gave her food."

Madison resisted the urge to snap at her that it hadn't been enough. She wouldn't care. "Can I hug her?"

"You're not getting anywhere near her until you tell me what you learned. Why did you want to meet?"

"Because they know I'm a spy for you," Madison told her.

He needed to make it believable. "They suspected before, but they're sure of it now. I heard two guards talk about it, so I know they would have gotten rid of me if I hadn't left. I want to come back, Fay. I've done everything you asked of me. I put myself in danger, and I could have died. Please."

"What else do you know about the pack?"

She wasn't going to let this go easily, which wasn't a surprise. "The pack is a mess. After everything that's happened, many people wonder if having Kieran as their alpha is a good thing. They'd been talking about removing him but don't know who could take his place."

Fay looked like a kid in a candy store. "I could."

Madison had to resist the urge to roll his eyes. "I'm sure most of them would be happy to have the option. They don't like what's happening, and they'll take pretty much anyone who promises to keep the pack out of trouble."

Fay's eyes narrowed, and Madison wondered if he'd gone too far. He probably shouldn't have said the pack would take anyone—that made it sound like she wouldn't be a good choice. Madison didn't care about hurting her feelings, but he did care about her not hurting Katie.

Fay smiled, and Madison's stomach churned. He didn't like how happy she looked, even though he was giving her what she wanted.

"I'll get the pack back, and I'm glad to hear that people want me as their alpha." She looked at Madison's father. "Do what you want. I have no use for them anymore."

With that, she turned and started walking away.

Katie took the opportunity to launch herself toward Madison, and even though their father tried to stop her, he was unable to.

But that didn't stop him. He was smiling as he moved toward Madison and Katie, almost as if he'd been looking forward to getting rid of them like Fay had ordered. His claws slid out as Madison watched him, a sure sign that his wolf was rising to the surface and that he'd use that form to kill them. When his fangs dropped and he snarled, Madison knew it was over.

For a second, Madison was terrified he and Katie were about to die. Then, seemingly out of nowhere, his guardian vampire appeared in front of him. Moving so swiftly Madison's father had no opportunity to try to fight or shift, Tyrian stood behind him and grabbed his head with both hands. "Let your children go," he demanded.

Madison's father snarled and started to turn. "Never. They're mine to do what I want with, and I have plans for them."

The crack of his neck when Tyrian broke it was loud and echoed against the walls of the empty motel.

The body dropped to the ground. For a second, Tyrian stared at it. He couldn't have avoided killing Madison's father when the man had refused to let Madison go, but what would happen now? Would Madison be able to forgive Tyrian?

Tyrian turned. Madison was crouched in front of his sister, and she'd buried her face against his neck. He was holding her tight and making sure she didn't look at their father, but he was staring with horror.

Tyrian took a step toward him, then stopped. How could Madison even look at him after what he'd done? He'd been protecting Madison and Katie, but to do so, he'd had to kill their father. How could anyone look at him with any emotion other than horror after that?

Something cracked under Tyrian's foot as he stepped back. Madison's gaze jerked to him, and for a moment, they stared at each other. It was good that Tyrian didn't need to breathe because he couldn't. The only thing he could do was wait for the moment Madison would scream at him for killing his father.

But Madison didn't. Instead, he got to his feet and hauled Katie into his arms. She was too big for that, but she wrapped her legs around his waist and clung on as if she was afraid to lose him again.

"We should take her home," Madison murmured.

Tyrian looked at the body on the ground. Someone needed to take care of it, and that someone should be him, but Madison had said *we*. He wanted to take Katie home and Tyrian to go with them.

Tyrian couldn't say no. Madison's father wouldn't be going anywhere, anyway. It didn't matter if they left him here or if Kieran wanted it dealt with. The body wasn't in pack territory, and from what Tyrian knew about the man, he didn't deserve any dignity. He wouldn't feel guilty about abandoning him there.

As long as Madison didn't care, either.

Tyrian quickly moved closer but hesitated to touch Madison because he didn't know if Madison wanted him to. Madison was focused on Katie, but his gaze kept flickering toward Tyrian until Tyrian couldn't stand it anymore. He put a hand on Madison's back and guided him toward the car, relieved when Madison didn't shy away from his touch.

Madison climbed into the back without letting go of his sister. He kept talking to her, and Tyrian felt he was intruding, so he focused on getting them back home.

He almost couldn't believe that the pack felt like home to him now. He supposed that as long as his family and Madison were with him, anywhere could be home, but he could see himself staying here for the long term and building a life he'd never thought he'd have. He could imagine him and Madison raising Katie together and maybe adding a few children to their family.

But that wouldn't happen if Madison hated Tyrian now.

Tyrian peered in the rearview mirror to see that Madison was looking back at him. Tyrian mouthed *I'm sorry* and prayed Madison would forgive him.

Madison smiled. "I don't care what you did, Tyrian. I have Katie back, and that's the only thing that matters."

"I'm still sorry."

"Well, I'm not, so stop beating yourself up. The world is a better place without him in it. Besides, he didn't give you a choice, and I'd rather have you in my life than him."

Tyrian could hear that Madison was telling the truth because it shone in his voice. He sighed in relief, and while the trouble wasn't over, at least for Madison and Katie, it was. They'd never have to be separated again.

Tyrian would make sure of that.

He was sure Katie was asleep by the time he parked the car in front of the house where he and Madison lived, along with his family. He quickly walked to the back door to take Katie and help Madison out of the car, but as soon as he touched her back, she cringed closer to Madison.

"I have her," Madison said.

Tyrian kept his distance because he didn't want to scare her. He could imagine everything she'd been through, and while she was with her brother now, she didn't know Tyrian. It was something they'd need to get over, but not now.

"This is Tyrian," Madison told his sister as they climbed out of the car.

Katie peeked at Tyrian, who smiled carefully to avoid exposing his fangs.

"He's my boyfriend," Madison continued.

Tyrian wasn't used to being anyone's boyfriend. The word felt too modern and like it didn't represent what he felt for Madison, but it was perfect to get Katie to understand.

"He's a vampire," Katie whispered.

"He is, but he's a good vampire. He got you away, didn't he?"

"He's not going to hurt me?"

"I promise he's not. He loves me, and he would never do anything to hurt me or you. I know you're scared, but you're safe now, and we're home."

That seemed to help her relax. She still clung to her brother, but Tyrian didn't expect her to be okay with everything that had happened anytime soon. He'd have to talk to Kieran about finding someone for her to talk to, but for now, she was safe and with her brother, and that was enough.

"I'll take her to my room," Madison said.

Tyrian nodded and stayed back. He sent a group text to his family so they'd know about Katie and to be careful with her. She'd be scared of them, but hopefully, not for long. Tyrian was ready to move out if it meant staying with Madison and Katie, but he didn't know if that was something Madison would want. They'd been sharing Tyrian's room recently, but Katie's presence could change everything.

He also made sure Parker and Yvonne had made it back. Parker confirmed they were fine, although he wasn't happy about not fighting at all. Tyrian could almost hear him whine through the text, which made him smile.

Once everyone knew about Katie, Tyrian headed to his room. He needed to shower after what had happened with Madison's father to get every trace of the man off his body.

He was stepping out of the shower when he heard a knock on his bedroom door. He wrapped his towel around his waist and went to open it, expecting one of his children.

It was Madison.

His cheeks flushed, but he didn't hesitate to push Tyrian into the room. The next thing Tyrian knew, Madison's arms were around his neck, and Madison was kissing him. Tyrian groaned and grabbed Madison's waist to haul him closer.

Madison clung to him, even when he moved him toward the bed. Tyrian wanted to ask him if he was sure, but he didn't dare. Madison had come to him. He knew what he was doing, and Tyrian needed to stop trying to protect Madison from himself when Madison had shown he was more than capable of doing so.

Tyrian moved Madison toward the bed, half carrying him until he could drop him there. Madison laughed. The sound was light and happy, something Madison hadn't had enough in his life. He looked so good spread out on Tyrian's bed like he belonged.

He did. Tyrian never wanted him to leave. He'd do anything to keep Madison in his life permanently, would promise anything. Madison was his future.

Madison pushed up to kiss Tyrian. Tyrian wanted to ask about Katie, but Madison wouldn't have left her alone if she'd needed him, so Tyrian wasn't worried.

He kissed down Madison's neck, then up to his mouth again because he didn't want Madison to feel uncomfortable. As he kissed him, he slid his hands under Madison's t-shirt and pushed it up until it got stuck under Madison's armpits. Madison huffed, and his impatience made Tyrian smile against his skin.

When Madison pushed Tyrian away, Tyrian knew it wasn't because he didn't want this, so he wasn't surprised when Madison pulled his t-shirt off and threw it across the room.

Now they were naked skin to naked skin, and Tyrian had never wanted anyone as much as he wanted Madison. It sounded corny and maybe like a lie since he was so old, but it was true. He'd never met anyone like Madison—someone who was a contrast of strength and weakness, someone who needed him as much as he needed them.

They kissed again. Tyrian stroked his fingertips down

Madison's chest and held him close, hooking his arm around his back. Madison wasn't going anywhere, but something in Tyrian needed the reassurance. He kissed down again, avoiding Madison's neck and aiming for his nipple. He didn't hesitate to suck and even gently bite down until Madison squirmed. Madison's cock tented his jeans, and while Tyrian wanted everything Madison was offering, he didn't want to rush.

He tried taking his time, but Madison was impatient, so it didn't last long. Madison eventually reached for the towel that was hanging on for dear life around Tyrian's waist. He grinned and unhooked it, then surprised Tyrian by rolling them until Tyrian was under him.

As soon as he was, Madison pushed his jeans down his legs. He wobbled as he tried to do that and go back to kissing Tyrian at the same time, but when Tyrian reached out to help him, he shook his head. Tyrian dropped his hand again and watched the show.

There was no finesse in the way Madison moved. He was too eager to get naked with Tyrian, and Tyrian didn't blame him because he wanted the same.

Madison finally managed to toss away his jeans, but he froze as if he didn't know what to do. His lips had parted, and he stared at Tyrian as if he didn't quite believe they were doing this.

He was gorgeous. He wasn't afraid like he'd been in the beginning. He wasn't as hesitant, either. He was taking what he wanted, and Tyrian loved it.

Madison finally moved again. His lips closed around Tyrian's cock, causing Tyrian to bite hard on his lower lip. There were people in the house, and he didn't want them to hear what was happening. He especially didn't want Katie to hear it, and her room was close by.

Madison's mouth was warm and welcoming, and while he

moved hesitantly, it was perfect. They'd talked, so Tyrian knew that while Madison wasn't a virgin, he also wasn't very experienced. Tyrian was humbled that Madison wanted this with him, of all people.

Madison looked at Tyrian the entire time he was sucking him off. Tyrian couldn't look away. Madison might not be experienced, but Tyrian was already about to explode just from having Madison's mouth on him, so he didn't need to be. Madison's hold on Tyrian's cock was strong and lovely — and driving Tyrian crazy.

He slapped a hand to the side, attempting to reach the nightstand. Luckily he was close enough to open the drawer, but it took him a few tries to find the lube. Once he did, he wasn't sure what to do with it, though. Who would be fucking who?

He didn't have to ask, because once again, Madison took charge. He usually didn't, but it seemed that in the bedroom, he enjoyed it, and Tyrian was delighted. He didn't mind keeping Madison safe while they were out there and having Madison make the decisions when it came to sex.

Madison let go of Tyrian's cock and flopped on the mattress next to him, stretching out on his stomach. He buried his face against his arms but peeked over them beseechingly with one eye. There was a request there, and Tyrian was happy to give Madison what he wanted.

Tyrian sat up, lube clutched in his hand. Madison opened his legs and hid his face against his arms, but Tyrian saw how flushed his cheeks were. He wanted to watch Madison's eyes as they did this, but they could do it that way later.

Tyrian had many, many plans when it came to the man he loved.

Tyrian settled between Madison's legs and opened the lube. He leaned forward to kiss Madison's back and shoulder as he slicked his fingers. Madison trembled under him, but

Tyrian trusted him to say something if it was too much, so he continued.

He rubbed his fingertips together to spread the lube, then reached between Madison's legs. Madison sighed, and his shoulders relaxed. He was surrendering to Tyrian. He trusted him to take care of him.

Tyrian was careful but thorough as he began stretching Madison. Madison's body made him want everything at once, but for Madison's sake, he took his time. He needed Madison to be ready, and he knew Madison was when he started shoving his ass back and whimpering. Tyrian twisted his fingers, and Madison pushed his knees under his body to rise.

It was time.

Tyrian slid his fingers out, and Madison whimpered again and pushed back. Tyrian quickly cleaned his hand, not caring about the sheet on the bed. He leaned over to kiss Madison's back as he took hold of his cock and aimed it at Madison's body.

Madison took him in like a dream. Tyrian slid into his body and let go of his cock to grab Madison's hips instead. He held Madison steady until he was fully inside of him and paused for a second, closing his eyes.

Madison was the only man he'd have in his bed from now on, and that was how he wanted it. Madison was his future, and Tyrian wouldn't have it any other way.

Tyrian leaned over Madison's body and kissed every inch of skin he could reach as he fucked him. When he snaked his hand around Madison's body to find his cock, Madison made a strangled sound and rose to his knees. Tyrian could only mirror his movement, even though he didn't understand why Madison was doing it. Maybe Madison's cock felt better like this.

Madison reached back and hooked a hand around Tyrian's neck. He pushed Tyrian's face against his neck, and Tyrian bit on his lower lip again.

"Bite me," Madison said.

Tyrian blinked, sure he'd heard that wrong. "What?"

"Bite me. I want to be the only person you'll bite from now on."

Tyrian hadn't expected Madison to want this, and he hoped neither of them would regret it. He didn't hesitate to obey Madison's order because he didn't want to. He yearned for what Madison was asking.

Madison tilted his head even more to the side, and Tyrian bit down. Madison cried out and shuddered, but he didn't try pulling away. Instead, he pushed his entire body against Tyrian's, silently telling Tyrian he wanted this.

The combination of sex and blood was heady, and it went straight to Tyrian's head. He sucked on Madison's neck and fucked him in unison, reducing Madison to a whimpering, needy man. His body tightened around Tyrian, and his cock jerked in Tyrian's hand, which told Tyrian all he needed to know.

Madison shuddered and thrust back one last time. His cock spurted all over Tyrian's hand, and the scent of Madison's pleasure, combined with his blood, pushed Tyrian into a frenzy he rarely felt. He fucked into Madison harder but stopped drinking from him because he couldn't coordinate anymore. Instead, he licked Madison's skin until he snapped his hips into him one last time and started filling his hole.

Madison whimpered again. Tyrian felt like a wet noodle, but as soon as he was back into himself, he carefully lowered Madison to the mattress. Madison allowed him to manhandle him.

"Are you comfortable?" Tyrian asked. His focus was drawn to the twin puncture marks on Madison's neck.

"Never better, and I mean that, so don't start obsessing over the biting thing. I wanted it."

"I did, too." But Tyrian would never have asked, and he suspected Madison knew that.

Madison reached for Tyrian. "Come here."

"We should clean up."

"As soon as my legs work again, we can shower together. Sorry I got you all dirty again."

Tyrian buried his face against Madison's neck. "You can get me dirty any time you want."

CHAPTER SEVEN

The sound of Katie laughing made Madison smile, and at the same time, it made his eyes burn.

He didn't want to cry, but he wasn't sure he could avoid it. How could he? He'd never expected to hear that sound again. He'd thought for sure that he'd lost his sister, even when she'd been in front of him, framed by Fay and their father. Madison had known Fay wouldn't make it easy on him, and he'd been right. She'd basically told Madison's father to kill both of his children, and he'd been about to do it.

That was one of the reasons Madison couldn't find it in himself to blame Tyrian for killing him. He was sure that Tyrian wondered if he should have given him a chance to change his mind, maybe to finally realize that he cared for his children, but he wouldn't have. Madison's father had never loved his children. Sometimes, Madison wondered why he'd even had them, but he thought he knew. It was what was done. Before Kieran, everyone in the pack was supposed to contribute, both with their work and by making the pack stronger and adding members. That was what Madison and Katie had been for their father. He'd been a horrible man, and the world was better without him.

It was certainly better for Madison and Katie. Katie was settling down, and while she'd initially been wary of the vampires, she'd relaxed and seemed to consider them family now. She had questions about Tyrian and how it was possible for him and Madison to be together, which had made Madison flush like a debutante. Katie had even more questions about

121

Tyrian being able to go out in the day, which Madison had been able to answer.

All in all, he was happy. He had Katie back, and she was safe. He had Tyrian, someone he'd never expected. He had a home with the pack, and people were finally starting to soften toward him, maybe because they'd seen Katie. A few people had come up to him and told him they were glad to see she was all right, and while he hadn't told them that she was the only reason he'd left the pack initially, he suspected they knew. They wouldn't bring it up, because they were ashamed of how they'd behaved, but that was fine with him.

He didn't care how others felt. He just cared that he and Katie were all right.

He looked at his sister. The family was watching a movie like they often did. Katie had been the one to choose it this time, and she'd chosen a live-action movie of a cartoon Madison remembered watching as a child. She was sitting between Yvonne and Meyer, who didn't seem to know what to do with a child. He was a bit stiff but smiling, and he kept peeking at Katie.

Once, Madison would have thought he was thinking about biting her, but he trusted every single vampire in the room never to hurt him or Katie. They were as safe as they could be, and Madison was able to relax.

Katie had only ever had him to keep her safe. That had changed. Now, she had a family of ten adult vampires to watch out for her. Madison would always worry about her, but he wouldn't worry about her safety anymore.

The arm Tyrian had wrapped around Madison's shoulders tightened as he pulled Madison closer. He wasn't paying attention to the movie, and Madison could feel his gaze on him.

He already knew what would happen next on the screen, so he didn't feel guilty about tilting his head up to look at the man he loved. "What?" he asked in a whisper.

Tyrian grinned. He'd been doing more of that since he'd realized Madison was comfortable with his fangs. It was still weird to think that he was and that Tyrian bit him regularly, but Madison loved it. He was the only one to feed the man he loved. He was the one who provided him with what he needed to survive, and it made him feel useful. Tyrian was a protector, and he'd make sure nothing happened to Katie and Madison. Madison had felt at a disadvantage because there wasn't anything he could offer in exchange, but now, he knew there was.

More than an exchange of things they could do for each other, he just enjoyed being bitten. They only did it when they were in bed together, and feeling Tyrian in him while his blood was in Tyrian was enough to make Madison shiver even now.

"What are you thinking about?" Tyrian asked.

Madison wasn't about to answer that question considering Tyrian's family surrounded them. He grinned, hoping it was enough for Tyrian to understand.

Tyrian's smile widened. "You naughty, lovely man. Why do you have to make me think about that when I can't have you?"

Madison wiggled closer to Tyrian. "Anticipation. I want to be sure you're ready for me once this is over."

"But don't you know? I'm always ready for you."

Madison shivered again at the promise in Tyrian's voice. He couldn't wait for the movie to be over.

He could have gotten to his feet and dragged Tyrian upstairs, but he didn't, no matter how much he wanted to. He enjoyed spending time with the family, especially since he hadn't had any of this when he was a child. It was good that Katie was now surrounded by uncles and aunts who would give her the love she deserved. That was all Madison wanted, but he was happy to realize they were also giving *him* love.

For now, they still lived together. The mess with the dragons and Fay wasn't over, and Madison couldn't see it ending anytime soon. There had been an uproar in the human world after the dragons had attacked the mall, but so far, they didn't know what was happening. They kept talking about the dragons as animals, and Madison hoped things would stay that way. It meant they weren't looking for humans, though. The clan wouldn't pay for what they'd done at the mall, and that didn't sit well with Madison.

The pack would have to step in. The supernatural world had been shaken by what the clan had done, and they were finally ready to work with Kieran and the pack. Together, they'd have to get rid of the clan because of how many people they'd killed and because they'd exposed their world to humans.

Madison was glad he didn't have to be involved in any of that. He wouldn't be the one making decisions, which was a relief, but he'd be there if anyone needed him. He and Katie were the only ones who'd left Fay, but unfortunately, there wasn't much he could tell Kieran about his sister. Madison didn't know where she was living now, and neither did Katie, since Fay moved around a lot. He didn't care, either. He wanted Fay to stay as far away from him and Katie as possible.

He didn't know what the future held, but he cherished everything he finally had. He'd fight like hell to make sure Katie and Tyrian made it through what was coming, along with the rest of Tyrian's family.

Because they were Madison's family now, too. They were as loyal to him as they were to Tyrian, and he was ready to protect them the same way they would protect him if he needed to be.

But the most important person in Madison's life, the one person he'd do anything for, was finally sitting in the room with him, laughing at the antics of the characters on the screen. Madison would fight like hell for Katie, but he'd fight even harder for Tyrian. Eventually, Katie would grow up and have her own life, but Madison's life was with Tyrian, and that was how he wanted it.

Now and forever.

ABOUT THE AUTHOR

Catherine is the creator of several series, most of them paranormal, including the Whitedell Pride Series and the Gillham Pack Series. While she graduated in translation, she decided to go the writer's way because it was more fun to create her own stories and characters.

She's been living in Italy for more than twenty years, but she's a daughter of the North—Belgium to be precise—and she misses it so much that she's already planning to move back.

She loves pizza—probably too much—her son, her pets, and of course, books. She sneaks some reading time into her schedule every time she has five minutes free from writing, demands from her various pets and son, and lastly, housework.

Connect with her:

lievens.catherine@gmail.com
BookBub: https://www.bookbub.com/authors/catherine-lievens
Website: https://authorcatherinelievens.com/
Facebook: https://www.facebook.com/catherine.lievens.9
Facebook Group: https://www.facebook.com/groups/411788002341528/
Twitter: https://twitter.com/authorCLievens
Newsletter: http://eepurl.com/c-uvKn